# DEEP OVERSTOCK
#18: Old Favorites
October 2022

> We don't need to have just one favorite. We keep adding favorites…. But we never lose the old favorites.
>
> *Lloyd Alexander*

## DISP - OLD FAVORITES

### Editorial

**Editors-In-Chief:** Mickey Collins & Robert Eversmann
**Managing Editors:** Michael Santiago & Z.B. Wagman
**Poetry:** Jihye Shin
**Prose:** Michael Santiago & Z.B. Wagman
**Cover:** Icons from IconScout
**Contact:** editors@deepoverstock.com
deepoverstock.com

# ON THE SHELVES

### SPACE EXPLORATION

8 on an otherwise unremarkable night by BEE LB

12 On Mining Station Gamma Twelve by Amalia E. Gnanadesikan

13 The First Astronauts by Daniel J. Nickolas

14 Rocket by Carolyn Adams

15 Future Astrophysicists of America, or, Children Staring Into a Void by Anna Laura Falvey

### FAIRY TALES, FABLES & FOLKTALES

18 Firebird by Audra Burwell

19 Survival Guide for Mortals Trapped in 2022 by Clarissa Grunwald

20 Spirulina by Riley Huff

21 The Lost Tribe by Caroline Reddy

23 Lowenna's Piskie by Kate Falvey

26 One Noble Neighbor by Ryan Shane Lopez

29 Trust by Anna Laura Falvey

### PARANORMAL ROMANCE

31 How to Make Love to a Female Human (Homo sapiens sapiens) by Karla Linn Merrifield

33 Queen of Diamonds by Carella Keil

35 What They Say about Big Feet by Vernon Tremor

39 Confessions at the Pantheon Bar by Ben Nardolilli

### NAUTICAL LORE

41 My Daughter Clare by Herma S.Y. Li

59 El Segundo, California by Fin Ryals

60 Sea Goddess by Justin Ratcliff

61 A Seaworthy Soul by Nicholas Yandell

64 Cora Visits the Seaweed Kingdom by Kate Falvey

67 Bearings by Alex Richardson

### DREAMS

69 I Know That If I Shrunk Down To Three Inches Tall My Cat by Cecily Cecil

70 Town of Dust by Audra Burwell

71 A Candle in the Window by Marie Dolores

75 Cum mortuis in lingua viva - A handover in letters by Lars Straehler-Pohl

82 The Train by A.R. Bender

93 Into which what follows by Carolyn Adams

94 Big Fish, Little Fish by Carolyn Adams

95 What do your dreams tell you? by Joan Mazza

### WESTERNS

97 Equus by Audra Burwell

98 I Will Never Be a Cowboy by BEE LB

*continued...*

*continued...*

## HORROR
101 Postcard From the Crypt by Deborah Coy
102 The Color of Light (Цвет света) by Ivan de Monbrison
104 Skull, Curiousity Shop window, Paris by Roger Camp
105 Tenuous Threads by Audra Burwell

## STRUCTURES
107 Book Sale by Christine Kwon
109 The Capitol Dome by Mark Parsons
112 Storms Over Red Wing by Carolyn Adams
113 Cliff Dwellers by Carolyn Adams
114 Oubliette by Justin Ratcliff

## NEW ARRIVALS
116 In the Attic by Alan Brickman
121 The Identity Card by Maumil Mehraj

## ORIGIN OF LIFE
126 The Eves by Olive Wexler
127 origin story by BEE LB
129 Conversations in a Graveyard by Daniel J. Nickolas
130 born by Clarissa Grunwald
131 Sand Mandala With Ancestral Names by Kate Falvey
132 Cremation by John Delaney

## ANIMALS
134 Self-Portrait as Angler Fish by Cecily Cecil
135 The Ape by Eric Thralby
136 The Return of the Ape by Eric Thralby
138 Chef, taxidermy shop by Roger Camp

139 Traces by Kate Falvey
142 Guest by Carolyn Adams
143 Part of Darkness by AJD

## MYSTERIES
151 The Loaf by Elizabeth Templeman
154 This Screaming Mad//man by BEE LB

## FUTURE
156 I Left Your Keys on the Kitchen Table by Carella Keil
157 my robot by Mark DeCarteret

## MAGIC
159 Ricky's Magic Powers by Alan Brickman
173 Igniting Moons, for You by Herma S.Y. Li
174 The Lion's Gate by Caroline Reddy

## SHAKESPEARE
176 Shakespeare in Winter by Lynette G. Esposito
177 My Cousin Shakespeare Said by Lynette G. Esposito

## SUPERHEROES
179 There's No Place Like Homophobia by Timothy Arliss OBrien
182 Mama's Little Angel by Z.B. Wagman

## BEEKEEPING
186 BB Keeping by Desiree Ducharme
193 XOXO, Candyman 2 by Heather Hambley

# Letter from the Editors

Dearest Readers,

So it's come to this: a *Deep Overstock* clip show. But this issue is more than just a rerun of all seventeen of our past themes. Contributors have not just resubmitted, but reinvented and reimagined these themes in new ways. This issue really is a collection of *new* favorites on old themes, but that doesn't really work as a title/theme.

We received over 260 pieces during our open submissions period and we wish we could have accepted more for this issue, but you might not have been able to pick it up! We even considered splitting the journal in two in order to to make it more accessible, but instead opted for this novel-length journal instead. (At this point, this seems more like an anthology than a "journal.")

A big thank you to all of our contributors for this issue. If we didn't accept your piece it was more likely an issue of space than of quality. We count ourselves lucky to have so many pieces to pick from.

And thank you, dear reader, for pulling us off the shelf and choosing to support *Deep Overstock*. We will continue to publish work that we don't see represented on the shelves in our next issue: Hacking. Give us ones and zeroes, axes, and writers who just can't cut it, or whatever else that "hacking" inspires in you.

We may not be the oldest journal out there, but hopefully we can be one of your favorites.


Until we're old and gray,

    Deep Overstock Editors

# DEEP PR  
# DO   E   R  
# OVE  
# STOCK

# SPACE EXPLORATION

# on an otherwise unremarkable night
## by BEE LB

the symphony of bugs buzzing around our bright
bodies. the spray acrid as gasoline over our arms,
legs, torsos, faces scrunched like zipper spokes.

the wind hesitating before reaching to touch
the leaves, our hair sticky with sweat being
lifted briefly before settling again. a reflection

telescope takes time to temperature adjust.
nothing to do but wait. look up. look around.
count seconds or blades of grass; it's all the same thing.

think, as always, of galileo. the slim aesthetic of a three-
legged refractor, retractable like spyglass. the sacrifices
we make for clarity, newton's cylindrical tube.

crosshairs the same as a shotgun,
though no risk for crossing deer. something
about it feels almost the same. maybe just

the empty field, the bright open sky, the bleeding
heat. hunting reminds me of nothing so much as sweat

trailing neck, hair clinging to slick skin, hands heavy,
swelling with heat. though i can't remember anymore
if i've really been. memory and truth do not always overlap.

like now, but not. the blind in the trees, watching dawn crawl
its way across the sky. the telescope on the ground, watching

sunset blink its heavy eyes to sleep. the telescope takes exactly as
much time to adjust as it takes to sink into the right trail of
thought.

tonight the sky is soft as silk, so few clouds to disrupt the sighting
it seems almost as if a spindle of fabric were rolled out across
the horizon. stars like jewels, or pinholes, and the whole sky

opening like the epitome of possibility.
there is something to be said about lenses adding ease
to the gift of sight, but i am not the one to say it.

i'll say instead: everything
reminds me of something else

and sliding the lens into place on the telescope feels exactly
like sliding the glass sample under a microscope.

the magnification of stars
and cells could not be less alike,

but the bloom of wonder is just the same.

crickets are singing their sweet song and when i remember
it is simply the brushing of legs, somehow, it grows sweeter.

there is no end to the joy of wonder.

the dial twists, untwists; the sky grows fainter, then sharper
closer, then farther; though nothing aside from sight

is changing. stars flicker
like camera spots, shining
then blurring then splitting

apart. focus is key, and with something so small as a star,
the key is elusive. the first star i caught in my sight was *vega*

the falling vulture, the year star,
judge of heaven, messenger of life.

the pleiades' predecessor once marked the start of a new year.
the sign that earth was once more ready to bear life, its fall
below the horizon unlocking the beginning of autumn.

all this, and too, named the most important star in the sky
save the sun. maybe that's why i called it my own,
the resonance of being second-best.

before polaris

was vega, north star, celestial navigator, axis-aligned,

ever-shining. in a future so distant it becomes
impossible to imagine, vega will reclaim its former
position: pole star, guiding principal, pre-eminent,
paramount. vega was traditionally named after

a loose transliteration: falling, landing.

at one time it was related to winter savory:
a bitter plant that flowers in summer, nearly
evergreen, less used than summer savory.

at the same time, it was related to olivine:
a mineral so easily weathered it's used to sequester
carbon dioxide; found in meteorites on our moon,
mars, infant stars, and a single asteroid discovered
the year i was born. its spectral signature has been seen
in dust disks around young stars, the tails of comets,
and the planetesimal belt around a single star,
the second-brightest in its constellation,
named painter's easel, larger and more
luminous than the sun.

the lockheed vega was named for my star,
and 5B was the plane Earhart took
as the first woman to fly solo
on a nonstop transatlantic flight,
five years before she disappeared.

the vega rocket began development the year i was born
and the first launch was set the day before
valentine's, the year i turned fourteen.

claiming something as your own is as easy as seeing it
and naming it *yours*. the way you say *shotgun*
when with a group of friends and you want,
for a moment, to feel special.

the way you see vega both in the sky above you,
with your own two eyes, a burning light so far you can't
understand—and in the glass below you, so close
your eyelashes brush the lens.

that feeling like you must be the first person
in the whole known universe to feel this way,
to feel this tug on your heart reminding you
of how big everything is and how miniscule
you are and how beautiful that realization is.

and though you know countless others have felt this way,
have put it to words better than you, and long, long before you,

somehow it feels *right* to see this star and name it *mine*
because you want, for a moment, to feel special.

# On Mining Station Gamma Twelve
by Amalia E. Gnanadesikan

Outside,
The sun has set,
The atmosphere is freezing
To the surface for the night,
While mining rovers trundle
Home through frosted
Regolith.

Inside,
The air ducts hum,
Recycled water flows through
Hydroponic gardens under lights.
A systems check confirms that
All is well inside
The airlock.

Elsewhere,
On Planet Earth,
It's said they walk on grass,
Enjoying sunshine as their right.

She sighs, and wonders
What it would be like
To go outside.

# The First Astronauts
## by Daniel J. Nickolas

Who are these determined apes,
    who endure
the cries of cracked bones
    and vertigo,
which precede the treetops?
Treetops where these apes
    reach and grasp
and check their fingertips to see
    if maybe
they'd grazed the halo.
They don't yet realize,
    yet still they reach
—unapologetically—
    up toward the twinkle
        which precedes the dawn

# Rocket
## by Carolyn Adams

Imagine a vehicle of dream and paradox,
where light is a force,
void is an entirety.
Imagine the improbability
of that.  How worlds
could extend that far.

You will travel a long time.

Track the closest body
to your window, watch it
enlarge to swallow its own
aura in a wild throat as it
slips past.  You're small,
an afterthought.  Still anchored
to gravity, you heed warning lights
that flutter instruments,
gauges that quantify the indistinct.
But you're already reaching
for the door.

There's an ache in your bones
for the dark outside your tiny home,
where Nyx unclothes.
You're almost
already gone.

And when you touch down,
bringing with you
the language and memory
of the thing you hope to be,
that first moment
in the wild enormity
will name you
for what you are.

# Future Astrophysicists of America, or, Children Staring Into a Void
by Anna Laura Falvey

When I was young, I stood on the hole
in the museum floor. The black seemed
unspecial, the dark inconspicuously final.
I stood and I watched the museum swallow
itself -- a world inverted, knotted, suffocated
and gone.

I watch

a little girl over the mouth of false infinite,
stepping lightly, drawn to it, I think, as I was
and am. She stepped onto it, stood for a moment,
and jumped:
a joyous and angry jump, shattering and powerful.
All ears rang and the stars rattled and then quieted.

a green shirt boy steps, steps off, steps again, falls,
and runs.

a boy and girl, slightly older, apprehensive, unimpressed.

a dinosaur shirt boy, dressed for the occasion, stood
and stared and jumped, knees high, power drunk.

a yellow dress girl stood stock still then took her doll, the softness
of which was evident, and placed it in front of her. She placed her
hand on its head, blessing, and pressed down, down until the body
was as flat as it could be. She did not push it through to the
other side.

a final total of hard jumps: 9

a boy with a dragon backpack backed definitely away
and walked carefully around.

a father, two sons, and a daughter wrapped together
balanced on one foot to fit.

a tranced, straight-backed, crane-necked, silent, tank-topped, fuzzy-sandaled girl stood for two tall minutes.

a buckled-sandal girl tipped her doll upside down
as if dipping her head systematically into a glass of milk.

a girl in a white ballerinas' skirt inches
forward until she jumps off.

a girl in a peasant blouse stood anchored,
stepped off, reconsidered, and left.

a sister hoisted a brother into the air
and he was weightless, tethered, looking down.

a boy in a shark shirt, thumb in mouth, sat
next to me, tapped on my shoulder, and said,

"look up."

# DEEP OVERSTOCK

## fairy tales, fables & folktales

# Firebird
## by Audra Burwell

Only in that sunless realm between asleep and awake
Will I find you, the shell of my former self, crumpled and
Lifeless, huddled in the darkest corner, two tattered wings
Sprouting from shriveled flesh, cracked and splintered
Like the decaying skin of a porcelain doll left forgotten.

I watch as you gracefully unfurl those battered wings, one
At a time, notes of dust cascading from the infinitesimal
Hairs lining their moth-eaten surface. A network of veins
Traverses them, like lightning shattered across the skin,
Electricity pooling in the beds of your nails, bitter and acrid.

Sparks emit from your wingtips, lighting up the room in a
Shower of white and blue flame, molten as it glides over
The ground, fingers of shimmering fire caressing your body
Like the ardent embrace of a lover, something you were
Cruelly deprived of in life, but have now mastered in death.

I watch as you begin to levitate, toes brushing the rotten floor.
You climb higher and higher, an incandescent glow forming
In your core, radiating outward, a magnetic ball of flame bracing
For eruption, as you are bathed in rebirth, rising from the ashes
Like a phoenix, the fabled firebird obscured by myth and legend.

An inferno dances in your eyes, two mirrors of the soul, sheathed
In broken glass, a reflection of myself staring back, as I feel the
Jagged and seeping chasm in my chest stitch itself closed, the
Needle guided by your hand, the thread spilling forth from your
Mouth, as we slowly merge, the past mending with the present.

# Survival Guide for Mortals Trapped in 2022
by Clarissa Grunwald

Be careful to whom you tell your true name.
Mind how the time moves--
one hour on Instagram is three in the real world.
Don't leave the path. Always ask for the price.
Then, ask again, just to be sure.
If you meet a man with the head of an ass,
leave Twitter as quickly as you politely can.
Where the maze burrows towards the future,
two brothers stand, guarding the exit. Remember:
Both can lie, or tell the truth.
This is not a riddle. Choose kindly,
and reach for a door.

# Spirulina
## by Riley Huff

She plays in the shallows, always just beneath the surface.

Find her near the mud banks of a shrunken lake. She is swimming among the weeds, happy to be free.

Nothing can move her. Not like it used to. She has felt her share of sadness and would rather keep her head up, locked on the sun.

She survives because of the sun, The Great Giver, The Cruel Taker, the light that shines over entire worlds. Water lets her breathe easy.

Water will never be pure again, but she has learned to tolerate the detritus in her home. Plastic containers and threatening blobs of waste and oil still float around her, whether she's stagnant as pond water or perfecting her backstroke.

But at last, no more will be added to the pile. The pipelines have stopped. The disposal has long ended. The toxins need to be broken down, but all that takes is time.

Everything decomposes over time.

She smiles more now, though no one can see her face. Her hair floats behind her, a carefree aquatic contrail.

The world is actually a beautiful place when you're not destroying it. And it's not destroying you.

Just open your eyes. She tells herself this every time she grows tired of dreaming. Breathe in deep. Look to the sun for enrichment. Know your responsibility to the world.

Because the world, as graceful a host as it may be, will always give back what it receives.

# The Lost Tribe
## by Caroline Reddy

I never knew that
the name Osei-Afrifa
was one of royalty,
until a classmate whispered:

you are of noble blood—

but I had been beaten
and belittled by so many
that I didn't believe


for years

I slept as until
I felt the stars of Anansi
and listened to
the *djembe* drum:

I danced
in the astral realm
and asked the Ashanti ancestors
to create a tapestry of kente cloth
so I could be clad in a regal robe.

I danced
in the astral realm
and asked the Ashanti elders
to create a ritual ceremony
as I cleared the battle fields.

I soared
above the prairies fields,
and sought the safaris
that could purify
the spears and swords.

I learned the ancient Akindra symbols
and sought the wisdom
that would to be sewn into my cells,

as I reclaimed my name: *Nana Aqua*
and the golden stool.

# Lowenna's Piskie
## by Kate Falvey

She liked the way I watched
the redstart work the berry
from the butcher's broom
and how I quieted my body
when the stoat poked its
twitchy whiskers from its den.

She liked when Mrs. Trengrouse
poked me with her hazel stick
while I crouched to see the pearls
on a fritillary feeding from a thistle
so I didn't hear her gwragh boots
frizzling the heath or the air shift
with the silent pinching of her cackle.

She liked the poke and how my eyes
poked back – but only underneath
my fluttered lids – and how I greeted
Mrs. T. as if meeting her for tea and
thanking her for pouring extra cream.

Then I saw a sudden blur of chert
and bramble spike into a stealthy dip
and snare of extra roughness beneath
the logan stones as Mrs. Trengrouse
humphed her mumbles toward
her stony ancient moss-ridden lair

and I was quick to her side
when she stumbled
and I walked with her to home
where I pillowed up her leg
and made her tea and she
even let me mother,
silly poking cow.

Dazy, she was, and no wonder, all her

sure-footed spite knocked out into
a wobble on a road she'd ever stomped
straight-backed and firmly down.
And when I went away

I said I would be back
with goosegrass for her scrapes
and an ear for her barking tales
of knockers,
devil's bargains, and the lady
of Dozmary Pool.

The light was leaving as I picked my way
through a drear and coming fog. I have eyes
like a beast cat's and the dark – even
after the old fool's bleddy lore – is no
enemy of mine but I know I am a girl
and not a mist and I know my wits and
steps can fail and falter when the path

is but a broth of vapor
and half-remembered goings-on.
A spark of song hatched from a shape
of crag and I saw – though how I saw
in so much dusky damp I never riddled out –

I saw a webby dress the color of tor and bracken
and a laugh the color of friendly stars.

They said I'd been gone for three full days
and that I looked well fed and scrubbed
with early morning sparkles.
No one seemed frantic when I woke
to faces peery in the logan stones
where they found me bedded in the heath.

But they did seem to keep away
even as they wrapped me in
some needless flurry of shawl
and shaken nerves. And I see her
in the skylark and the warbler and the snipe
and in all the fissured gestures of the stones,
and sometimes without warning

she resolves into a poke between
my heedless shoulders as I'm lulled
into the sedge and boggled grasses
after butterfly or vole
and reminds me of the iridescent

spreading of my own
gawky, rugged, pearly, earthen wings.

# One Noble Neighbor
## by Ryan Shane Lopez

From Grimm's *Little Red Cap*, Perrault's *Little Red Riding Hood*, & Christ's Parable of The Good Samaritan

There was once a sweet young girl who lived deep in the woods with her mother. Everyone who saw this girl instantly adored her. One day, her mother was feeling ill, so she gave the girl her coin purse, her riding hood, and her mule, and sent her into town to buy some cake and wine.

Along the way, the girl passed a meadow where a patch of beautiful sunflowers was in bloom. Unable to resist, she dismounted and began to pick a bouquet to lift her dear mother's spirits. Just then, a band of men came riding by and stopped to ask the young girl where she was going all alone. Not knowing it was unwise to speak to strange men, she held up her coin purse and told them she was heading into town to buy cake and wine for her sick mother.

"Does your mother live nearby?" they asked her.

"Not so near," answered the girl, "for it is a half day's journey to town and I have come three-quarters of the way already."

"And did you leave no one behind to look after her?"

"No one," admitted the girl, hoping the men were offering to check in on her poor mother, "for we live alone."

Seeing there was no one in sight, the men set upon the girl. They emptied her coin purse, stole her mule, and stripped off her clothing. When they had taken all they desired, they covered her with her mother's cloak and left her lying among the trampled sunflowers.

After some time, an old woman who lived in a nearby cottage came shuffling down the road, carrying a basket of freshly picked berries. When she saw the young girl cowering beneath a riding cloak, soaked red with blood, the old woman clutched her basket and hurried along on the far side of the road.

Next, a man who'd been cutting wood nearby came strolling down the road, whistling and carrying his ax over his shoulder. When he heard the little girl whimpering and begging for help, the woodcutter whistled all the louder and sauntered by on the far side of the road.

As night fell, the girl began to shiver with cold. Too weak even to stand, she began to cry out and, without knowing why, found she was calling the name of her own father whom she had not seen for many years. She had not been calling for him long when she saw two enormous yellow eyes peering at her out of the dark woods on the far side of the road. She trembled with fear as an old shaggy wolf crept out of the shadows into the moonlit meadow.

*I will never see my beloved mother again, thought the girl, for my foolish cries have brought a wolf here to devour me.*

The wolf circled her, sniffing her wounds, but did not devour her. Instead, it hoisted her onto its back and carried her off through the darkness. The girl, now quite delirious, imagined that the wolf was not a wolf at all, but her father who, hearing her cries across mountains and oceans, had flown to her side in her time of deepest need.

As she rode on his back, she spoke with him:

"Oh, Father, what big ears you have!"

"All the better to hear your cries for help, my child."

"And what strong legs you have!"

"All the better to carry you with, my child."

"And what thick hair you have!"

"All the better to warm you with, my child."

"And what sharp teeth you have!"

"All the better to protect you with, for these woods are crawling with wicked men."

When he reached a nearby cottage, the wolf pulled the bobbin with his teeth and the latch lifted. Once inside, he cleaned and bandaged the girl's wounds, pouring on oil and wine. Then, he dressed her in a nightgown he found, placed her in the bed beneath the covers, and drew the curtains. Despite his innate fear of the flame, he lit a fire to warm her. As she slept, he went out and caught a squirrel. He filled a pot with water from the well out back, skinned and gutted his catch, and cooked a stew over the fire. He sat on his haunches at the girl's bedside until the sun rose next morning, when he was relieved to see the girl's color had improved and she was able to take some of the stew he'd prepared.

Around midday, the wolf was changing the girl's bandages when, in through the door, walked the owner of the cottage, the very same old woman who had passed by on the far side of the road. One look at the wild beast, crouching over the half-naked girl and licking her wounds, and the old woman ran screaming all the way back to town.

Knowing this would mean trouble, the wise old wolf told the girl he must leave her now. But, calling him Father, she begged him to stay by her side.

That very evening, the old woman returned with the woodcutter to find the shaggy gray wolf still on his haunches at the girl's bedside. The beast did not snarl or snap or run. Even so, the woodcutter swung his ax and cleaved the wolf's head from its body with one blow. Then, he carried the girl back to her mother's cottage.

Afterwards, the tale spread far and wide of how the woodcutter had saved both an old woman and a little girl from the belly of the crafty wolf. Over the course of its many tellings, certain details were lost while others were altered and then altered again. But everywhere the tale was told, its hearers praised the woodcutter's courage and cursed the wolf's wickedness.

# Trust
## by Anna Laura Falvey

My mother always tells me, *you've got to pick your gods.*
She says this, leaning at a crow's angle over a cup of coffee,
a glass of wine, through the oiled steam of a stir fried dinner;

from under the tumble of her quilted bedclothes,
voice muffled behind a peeling murder mystery;
shouted out the back door to the forest before the dead bolt

has been undone. *If you worship false gods*, she says,
*your bones and your eyes and your mind will brittle
and fall away into nothing.* I imagine her sometimes,

tending a garden of nothing, the grave keeper
of false god worshippers: either with her hair gray
and middle parted, short and severe, lips pursed

in a respectful red line as she tends, or with a long
white braid down her back that persists, swinging
over her shoulder and into the earth. Here, she weeps

and laughs and the weeds tremble. She salts the garden
which burns through the molten remnants.
She says, through the acid hiss of pain dissolving,

*you've got to pick your gods.*

# DEEP DOVES OVERSTOCK PEEPER

**PARANORMAL R♥MANCE**

# How to Make Love to a Female Human (Homo sapiens sapiens):
## A Mini-Manual for Morphologically-Compatible Aliens or Undiscovered Extant Species of Hominids
by Karla Linn Merrifield

<u>Hold Hands</u>

Fingers laced
       grasp of trust—
              affection

<u>Hug, aka Embrace</u>

Encircle    enwrap arms firmly
      press bodies firmly—
           nuzzle clavicles

<u>On Love's Highest Art: The Kiss</u>

Study first her lips with your lips
      only then slip tongues gingerly

(for further study google search
Roy Lichtenstein *Kiss II* 1964)

<u>Re: Cunnilingus #1</u>

Watch 30 pussy massage porn vids
      (with guaranteed real orgasms*)
         how long does it take

on average to get her off
      remember that   allow for
        variation when practicing
*See below.

Re: Cunnilingus #2

In languor linger there on her
      as if there were no other world
           no tomorrow

Smack that Pretty Ass

Give that percussive thwack—
      get that hand print in pink—

Collect Reward

Having given    the receiving—
      good head to your godhead


Coitus/Intercourse/F*cking, Etc.

So many ways to say it on this Earth
      so many ways to do it in our Universe

Ask her how she first desires the penetration of bodies
      the interpenetration of minds unfathomable


O as in Orgasm

When it all comes down
      what it comes down to—
          *Holy f\*ck*

# Queen of Diamonds
## by Carella Keil

The soul of each moment is alive. A living voice, a broken down song. Like an abandoned car in an alleyway, from another life you've lived. Within another's ghost towns.

\* \* \*

"The most beautiful thing about you, is that you're strong enough to be vulnerable."

(Fuck you).

"The ugliest thing about you, is that you're weak enough to be impenetrable."

If I could break into your mind (love) like a shattered vase, I'd find no water on the floor.

I spilled too many of my flowers at your feet, thirsting for the voice and breath I'd given you.

Silence. You're the profound silence from the bottom of a well many women fall into, seeking the fragile child only to find a Black Sun staring down upon them, laughing.

Your little boy is an illusion, a mirage the Queen of Hearts stole a piece of to complete her own, and you believed it, you actually believed that love is a finite thing, and petals can't grow from stone, and floors must always be washed clean of dirt.

Memory is a sin and a stain, but you remember every fingerprint, catalogued in a desk of drawers next to a collection of video games and pornography, and stamps to worlds you're too afraid to travel to, lest you should leave some piece of yourself behind.

The White Pawn was your pass, the Black Bishop your port. And yet, you are a grown man hiding within a child's fort.

I am no better, with curtains for eyes and a home inside built on dreams as fragile as a web of tears.

Blow them away, love. Wipe the dust off your radiator, and watch all the women you've buried your head in drive past in their sleek cars, out your window frame, your standing-still-moving picture, and beyond the eclipse of your White Knight.

Black Bishop, White King. Black Pawn, Yellow Rose. Friendship is a hard thing to come by, in this land of salted flowers; and real love, harder still.

Tomorrow, I may write of the Crocodile and his tears, the Cowardly Lion and fields of rippling poppies in a sea bleeding with dreams. Or perhaps I'll scale a different rainbow, find marigolds and lavender and sunshine. I'll write forever. After all, words are the only thing left of us once we've turned to Stone.

Sincerely, the Queen of Diamonds, from the bottom of her cavern, Spade in hand.

# What They Say about Big Feet

## by Vernon Tremor

I have accepted that in this life I have a physical body and that I pushed it to extremes. I am a three-time Mr. Cascade and twice Eagle. I have dragged semi-trucks. And I have held airplanes back from flying.

But there has always been something missing.

When people tell me Bigfoot doesn't exist, I feel ropes tied around me and cinched. I feel the airplanes bucking and no matter what I do, no matter how hard I flex and keep my muscles tight, they fly away and tear my arms apart. I have dreams about this. And this is ridiculous, I know, but I often feel like if Bigfoot doesn't exist, I don't exist.

I have lost friends, lost jobs. I have had to change gyms. You cannot say directly that you believe. You must say you are 'open to the possibility.'

For me, Sasquatch is a n indisputable fact. The fact of him is as foundational to my existence as the adductors, the hamstrings, and glutes. When I hear, "Bigfoot isn't real" or "There's no squatch" or "You must be fucking nuts," I feel I am turned into a shadow.

I have felt his presence definitively only once. It felt what a hammer must feel when it first strikes a nail. In a flash, I knew who I was. It happened when I was a boy scout many years ago.

Our scoutmaster drove us into the mountain. It was a test of our individual survival capabilities, not of cooperation. We were to survive alone in the wilderness for a single night.

I built my camp beneath an enormous pine. *How strong it was!* From where I stood, I could not see its top. *How long its roots must be!* I unfolded my tent from my backpack and installed the skeleton-like frame. I pounded in the stakes and stretched the tent taut.

Establishing my sleeping bag, a book, and my battery lantern inside the tent, I came back out to stare into the dark limbs of the trees and see if I could spot a star. But the night was very dark. It was like walking into a cave inside a mountain. It was so black. I clicked the flashlight on and, in the flashlight light, I saw only the ferns, illuminated in light and dark shadow.

I looked into the forest, and pretended that I was not afraid. From my throat down to my heels, I was trembling.

That night I had a dream. It was a dream of sensation only. I saw nothing, said nothing, felt nothing save the sole sensation that the entire forest was chasing me. Then the sensation erupted into an all-pervading smell of forest, of fir trees, mud, and ravenous wild animals.

When I woke up in my tent, my member was stuck to my hand. It had never happened before. It was on my arm and my sleeping bag and my stomach. It clung to me, stuck to me, I was a mess inside it. I took a spare shirt and wiped it away. I wiped at it and wiped at it but it would not leave me.

The scout master was coming this morning to check on us. He would be pulling up to the parking lot any minute.

*If he came; if he shook my hand!* When I put my hand into his, I would be pulled into adulthood. Only now—now my hand was covered in my own terrible mess.

I unzipped my tent and fell out like spiders were chasing me. I ran to the stream, left my clothes on the bank, and jumped in. But, in the extreme cold as I rubbed my hands together, it still stuck to my hands. I pulled them out of the stream and stared at them in the fleeing darkness. It was like they were covered in sap.

A branch cracked in the trees.

"Is– is there someone there?" I said. "Scoutmaster?"

Something moved. Something breathed.

My body trembled as if I would die. I grabbed my clothes and ran back into my tent.

Wrapped in my sleeping back, I listened intently. I heard the general racket of trees and the rare whisper of animals, but nothing as intense as what I had heard in the stream.

That morning, I shook the scoutmaster's hand. Could he detect it? Could he feel what I had done?


It has been years since that first incident in the woods and I have since become bigger and bigger. Daily, I force my body into extreme biological violence, tearing my triceps, biceps, and lats until I finally feel myself undoubtedly deep in the world.

Still, ever after that one glimmer of hope, there has always been something missing, something I feel my very blood is in search of every night.

I have learned not to talk about Bigfoot. I have seen the recognition of friendship drift away from people's eyes. How do I dip my fingers into the great pool of love when I believe that cryptids walk the earth?

I have a body like a Volkswagen bus, and no one onto which I can foist it.

Still, to me, there is a heart always beating, waiting for my own heart to beat alongside it. It is as if they communicate, beating through the night like a radio signal. Our two distant hearts beating to find one another's frequency. Every night when I sleep, I drift again into the forest—heavy musk; enormous presence.

Since about a month ago, I have taken to jogging nightly in the woods behind my house. I have found little things, like little tufts of hair that cling high on the trunks of trees. A bear, or a cougar maybe? I plucked some down and rubbed it between my fingers. Still, I couldn't be sure.

One night, I thought I saw something impossible a ways off the path. The coldness was thick, as we were on the edge of October. Small wisps of fog crept among the trees. I slowed my pace down until I came to a stop. As it was about twenty-five yards off from where I stood, I could not see it well enough from the trail, and I abandoned the trail to run between the ferns until I got to it. I ran off the trail and into the woods.

I felt the sudden sense that again I wasn't alone.

"Is there someone out there?" I said.

Branches cracked behind the trees.

"I'm not afraid," I said.

The same smell, that same pervasive density, the scent of fir trees, thick mud, and ravenous wild animals.

It was like deadlifting to fail, then pushing beyond. Something inside me screamed for release.

Something moved. Something breathed.

A pair of hands so enormous they could close around a tree trunk appeared from the leaves. A tender voice so inflamed it was almost human. I cannot describe my thrill at those gargantuan feet. And you know what they say about big feet.

I exhaled and could see my own breath.

The creature came forward with a moan. The moan I had heard in my dreams, my dark dreams of impression and touch. How deeply it smelled of the woods. I trailed my fingers in his fur. In every conceivable way, his body was bigger than mine.

This time—

This time, I didn't run.

# Confessions at the Pantheon Bar
## by Ben Nardolilli

The bar attracts its failures, the strangest get in free,
one man calls himself the infectious consonant,
he cancels every engagement, blaming his grandmother's face,
and nothing sickens him
except the nausea he gets when looking at thorns

The black and white lips by the jukebox
spray out a bond of laughter,
they belong to a woman who urges us to buy her candles,
then her sleeping book, where we will come
to believe in the power of flowers in an ambitious agent's
handset

Meanwhile, the aged singer waits, she lives
in an instrument broken beyond mummification,
her friends will come under the neon canopy at midnight
to bring her another boy full of damage, yet
they will ruin one another swimming through his nightmares

# My Daughter Clare
## by Herma S.Y. Li

I can forgive myself for leaving him where he was, but I can't forgive myself for spending one whole year in depressed rage, forbidding anyone from saying her name in front of me. For three hundred and sixty-seven days and nights I lived in a world washed free of colors and joy, praying to the Gods of the Highlands that she could finally come to see the wrong she'd done, that she should come back to me. I prayed for her to return and know she had brought tears to my eyes and illness that was born from grief to her father, my husband.

I hate myself for it. And that hate would remain within my veins for as long as I lived, running through my blood with every thump of the heart.

\* \* \* \* \*

There were barely any traces that could be followed, but I still spent two years looking, searching. I found him in the end, near the borders of the Lowlands.

It was an early morning in late spring. His house had walls paved with rough gray stone, standing tall and fine between the curve of two grassy hills, and the air carried the scent of dew on grass. The hem of my traveling cloak dripped with rainwater from the night before as I approached it.

A boy who looked about nine or ten years old crouched near the front door of the house, collecting tangled bits of wool into a small basket. The wool was thick and curly, hidden between the outstretched branches of a short bush that had almost no leaves. He was so engrossed in the work that he didn't notice me.

"Pleasant morning," I said.

He jumped a bit and looked up, eyes wide as if I had come

right out of thin air. The half-filled basket hung from the crook of his left arm.

"I am light on my feet," I said. "Is this the house of Randy Hansen?"

The boy nodded and rose to his feet. He was about half a head shorter than me and tilted his face upwards slightly to give me a curious look. "I am Randy Hansen."

"I see," I said. "Is there anyone else here named Randy Hansen? I'm quite sure that I'm looking for an adult."

The boy frowned slightly, his basket of wool swinging almost undetectably in the lukewarm breeze.

"Your father, perhaps?" I prompted. "May I please speak with him? It would only take a moment."

The boy blinked twice. "Who are you?"

"A petite woman traveling around the place. I'm here for Randy Hansen," I said.

"Why are you looking for him?" the boy asked curiously, and then, after a few seconds of hesitation, added, "Why are you so tiny?"

"I have something to ask your father for help," I told the boy. "And being tiny isn't always a bad thing, young Randy. In my theory, people communicate better with those who are about the same height as themselves. My height lets me understand children better. I literally see things from their point of view."

The boy laughed, then said, "Wait here for a minute."

\* \* \* \* \*

I stood by the grassy hillside as Randy Hansen Junior went into the front door of the house. The house was larger than what most could afford these days. If I didn't know better I'd have thought it was the home of an old doctor or a lawyer, not the property of a former rogue.

The boy came back with a tall man who had broad shoulders and rough hair the color of clouds before a storm. He looked like he was somewhere in his thirties, striding across the calf-length grass.

"Well, hello," I said.

He didn't reply and instead stared at me distrustfully, his gaze moving from my auburn hair, which was a bit of a mess, to the hem of my tattered, dampened cloak.

"I'm looking for a man named Randy Hansen. If you happen to be him, please let me know. If you happen to not be him, please let me know, too, and I'll leave right away."

"And exactly why are you looking for Randy Hansen?" the man asked. His voice was low, like a rumble that comes from the back of a wolf's throat.

"I wish to hire him to be my guide."

"A guide," he repeated. "A guide to where?"

I looked directly at him. "It's hard to express through words, because you can't find it on a map. Some think the place doesn't exist. I mean a cave, on Rowk Island, in the mountains, or so I heard."

For a moment he fell silent, then called, "Randy, you go back inside the house."

"What? But dad—"

"Go. Don't make me tell you twice."

"But I want to know—"

The man slapped his son across the face. The sound of it broke through the thin sheet of silence that had covered over the hills of springtime.

"Go," he said.

The boy turned and dashed towards the house, almost tripping on his own foot several times along the way. A flap of the back of his shirt flew off his skin, and I saw bruises both green and purple, one atop another, for one brief moment before he reached the front door and hurried inside.

Randy Hansen turned back to me as if nothing happened and asked, "Why are you looking for the Cave?"

"I need money," I said bluntly. "And I heard the cave is full of gold. I want, no, I need that gold."

He looked me up and down and I waited for him to make a comment on my height, but he didn't. "I don't help people for free."

"That, I know," I told him as I reached into the pocket of my tunic and pulled out a leather bag and held it out. As he took the bag and opened it, pouring a handful of fat, round coins into the palm of his left hand I said, "Those are for the trip to the place. When we come back, I'll pay you double."

He nodded curtly and closed the bag once more, then said, "When we arrive at the Cave, I'm not going inside. You have to go by yourself, and you will be only allowed to take what gold you can carry on your person. I wouldn't touch them. The place's cursed."

"That's fine for me," I said.

He stared at me for a while, then said, "Fine. I'll go and grab some supplies for the trip. Wait here."

\* \* \* \* \*

We didn't say a word to each other during the first day of our journey, because both of us knew the way to Rowk Island. What I didn't know was the way up the mountain. The sky was a really soft purple as we walked on, climbing over hills and small mountains, and the temperature dropped as the sun set.

We met little people along the way. I made a fire, and both Hansen and I threw a handful of oats into the small pot of river-water an old gypsy woman gave us to cook. His handful was a lot of oats, while mine was only a small amount the size of my palm. He noticed this and said, "You'd better not be eating half the porridge."

I told him that I wouldn't, and I really didn't. It was another advantage of having a small frame. I eat much less than an average adult, which meant I could keep on traveling with a bit of wild berries and a few squirrels. I gave some food to the gypsy woman and she, in return, offered to see our palms and tell us our fortunes.

She took Hansen's hand first and looked closely at his rough palm. "You have come back to where you began," she said. "You will climb up to a high place….yes, you will….and, yes….something from your past is making its way back. It will find you."

He grunted, but I saw him steal a quick glance in my direction.

The woman took my hand next. I saw her wrinkled fingers, thin with age, trace the lines in my upturned palm. She was silent for a few moments before saying, "I see….oh yes, I see….there is death in your future, young lady."

"Death lies in every soul's future," I said.

I wasn't sure if she heard me or not. She studied my palm closely and didn't say a word. The winds of nighttime soared around the three of us as the woman spoke in a low whisper so that only I could hear her. "In your past, there was a girl in a tree; in your future, there will be a man in a tree."

I looked up at the gypsy woman and knew that she knew.

* * * * *

The next morning we set off early, climbing over the last few grassy hills. The sunrise spilled golden specks on the narrow roads and on our backs as we walked. Hansen was much taller than me, but didn't slow down even for a little bit, taking one big stride after another as I jogged to catch up. I didn't mind. The times jogging along hillsides with grass brushing against my pant legs reminded me of my own childhood, when I had to herd the sheep my family kept to the other side of the Highlands where there was the freshest water and plants for the sheep to feed on. We all need certain things to sustain our lives, I suppose. It reminded me of my daughter's childhood. Clare and I used to go for walks around the Highlands, and she would talk on and on about the boys in the village, her dream of being a dancer when she grew up, and the sounds the Highland winds made as they swept through the land, all over the place. Clare heard music in the wind in a way I never could. She said it was a natural thing—the dances, the movements, and the melodies came to her the way sheep came to their shepherd. Clare looked up at me and grinned, her auburn hair identical to mine a bit plastered to the side of her face. She liked sheep and rabbits, furry things with pure minds that munched on grass. She liked dawn and the full moon, bright orbs with light that watched over us. She liked the wool cardigan I made her, liked stories about magic and adventures, liked jam on her bread better than butter, liked the squishy armchair in our living room that was made by my husband a few weeks after she was born.

My only daughter, Clare.

\* \* \* \* \*

We got to the only pier in both the Highlands and Lowlands in the afternoon. The sea was a rusty gray, with white seafoam occasionally blooming over the top of the tides. I could make out the blurry outline of a piece of land a far distance away, covered in layered mist. Hansen saw it, too, and told me while pointing at the island, "There it is. Rowk Island."

I nodded. "Where the gold is."

"If we find it," he corrected me.

"How many times have you been there?"

"Only once." He pursed his lips. "Thought it was a legend, but I tried looking for the cave of gold, and I found it. I took what gold I could carry on my person and left Rowk Island.

Now get moving, do you plan to stand here till sunset?"

There were only a few fragile-looking wooden boats floating unsteadily in the flows of sea water, tied to the trunk of a withered tree. A rusted bell that was about the size of my fist hung at the end of a string tied to the only protruding twig on the tree's side, shivering in the wind.

I rang the bell, and soon after the metallic ring a fisherman, whose beard looked like an angry tangle of seaweed, hurried to our side, his voice hoarse as if he hadn't spoken in a long while as he asked, "Where to?"

Hansen and I boarded the small boat as the fisherman untied the rope which bound our boat to the dead tree. Sometimes you must leave the dead behind to move on. Speckles of rough sea-salt made soft noises as my boots stepped on them. The sky was a pale gray, like ashes left behind after the flames died out.

Water splashed into our boat as we sailed slowly forward. The fisherman held out his hand. "Three coins for an adult. As for you, young lass….one coin should do."

Hansen grumbled under his breath as he handed the man three coins. I, too, handed out three coins, knowing the fisherman had mistaken me for a child or a teenage girl due to my petite frame. He glanced down at my upturned palm which held the coins, then cackled loudly, "You didn't try to deceive me. Save the two coins. In times like this, two coins may help you do a lot more than taking a boat to an island with nothing but a mountain and loads of fog."

The boat rocked gently as I said, "Two coins are good, but I heard there's gold on Rowk Island."

Out of the corner of my eye, I saw Hansen shoot a warning look at me with a firm shake of his head. The fisherman turned to stare at me with wide eyes. "You're not looking for the Cave, are you?"

"You know about it?"

"Everyone around 'ere knows 'bout it," he said as a deep

frown creased his sun-tanned forehead. "And we know enough 'bout that blasted place to not go looking for it. You're an honest person, young miss. Don't go there. The place's cursed and it decays people's souls."

"I've heard the saying that gold decays human souls," I said, ignoring Hansen whose mouth was pressed into such a thin line his lower lip had gone pale.

The fisherman spat into the waves below. "Not the gold. The Cave *itself*. Who knows what the heck lives inside. The curse decays whatever happiness you thought you'd get from what you took from the Cave. You get a shitload of gold, yet whatever you buy with that gold cannot make you happy."

With that, he fell silent, and we sailed the rest of the way to Rowk Island with only the sound of water thrashing against the side of our boat.

* * * * *

Hansen and I left a trail of murky footprints on the onyx sand as we walked across the beach of Rowk Island. The tide rushed in to smooth our footprints away, leaving only wet glittery sand. White mist curled around everything, some patches of them so dense I felt it brush against my face like a shroud.

A shop run by a small family sat at the foot of Mount Mirk, and we filled our pockets with dried oats and jerky made from unknown large animals. Might be deer, or a goat, I wasn't sure. The youngest child in their family thought I was about her age—twelve or thirteen, at most—and waved at me with a smile. Her twin brothers ran around the store, passing a wooden ball around and laughing loudly, until their father yelled from behind the counter to scold them.

We left the store, and began our climb up Mount Mirk. Clouds and mist swirled on the path in dancing shades of gray and white, weaving in and out of one another. Hansen walked with big strides as if we were in a hurry, as drizzle began moistening the top of our heads. It was almost midnight when we made camp near a small pond. We made a fire to warm ourselves and to roast a fish I caught from the pond, as Hansen began tearing a large piece of jerky apart in a wolfish manner. Smoke from our campfire rose into the night sky, mingling with the mist which this island seemed to naturally produce. We slept atop a pile of dried leaves, me tugging my tattered cloak around myself to keep out the chill.

In the morning, I made some oats into porridge for breakfast, and we ate in silence as huge eagles circled high above us, their feathers blown wild by the strong wind. As they circled higher they became distant dots in the white daylight, like dreams that fade from our consciousness before people could remember them.

Hansen strode next to me, squishing nameless ferns under his boots. I looked up, squinting to see through the mist. From this angle, Mount Mirk looked like it rested its tip against the sky in the manner a writer would pause his pen above a page.

"How much longer till the Cave?" I asked.

"One day more, or maybe two, if it rains."

It started raining in mid-day, and gray vapor blanketed our surroundings, making the stones slippery and forcing us to slow down. We walked along a thin path that was probably used mostly by goats, which was fine for me but way too narrow for Hansen. He slipped on a particularly fragile piece of rock which crumbled under his weight and fell to the ground, his back slamming into the blade-like rocky landscape of the area. The blade-shaped rock went through his shirt, but didn't stab through his shoulder as it should have. Instead, the rock broke off when it came into contact with a sheet of armor he wore beneath, leaving Hansen unharmed but scowling, cursing the weather. I held out a hand to help him up, but he ignored me.

"Nice armor," I commented.

Hansen shook water from his rough hair before answering, "Snatched it with the gold from that cave years ago. Supposed to block every weapon there is."

"I thought there's only gold in the Cave," I said, though I already knew the answer.

Hansen shrugged. "The Cave provides what you want. I wanted gold and protection, and it presented me with that armor. The thing's unbreakable."

"What do you want protection from?"

"Anyone, everyone. Obviously," he snapped at me impatiently. "A man with gold is always in danger."

It was my turn to shrug, and we walked in silence the rest of the day. As we walked I looked around to remember the directions, marking out certain rocks and a few trees. We went up a steep slope when I saw a pile of goat bones, crossed a small stream which ran quick and shallow, walked along a second one until we reached a pile of rocks darker in color than the rest and turned left. We kept walking.

We made camp in a clearing and had some jerky as dinner, because there wasn't enough dry wood to make a fire this high up the mountain.

I was surprised when Hansen spoke.

"Why do you want gold?" he asked through a mouthful of jerky, chewing loudly in a way that would make any mother scold their child if they did the same.

"Why wouldn't I want gold?" I threw the question back at him, dumping some gravel out of my left boot.

He scowled at me. "You're a woman. Not an attractive one, but a woman nonetheless. Don't you have a husband to make the money you need? Or a son who works?"

"My husband died two years ago," I said. "Deadly disease, rough winter. He didn't make it through."

Hansen made a non-committal sound. I was glad he didn't tell me he's sorry. Most people with decent manners say that, but I've heard the sentence enough times in my life and didn't wish to hear it anymore.

I thought the conversation was over until he spoke again. "Was your husband short like you?"

I wasn't sure if the question was meant to sound offensive or if it just happened to be. "No, he was about as tall as you are. When we were young, some considered him the most handsome man in the Highlands. He got hundreds of sheep and a house from his family when he was old enough to leave home and to roam the world."

Hansen seemed speechless for a moment before he asked, "How come he married you?"

I told him the truth, "He said that I am intelligent and always reliable. Most importantly—I wanted him. I always get what I want. In the end, at least."

"But he died."

"We all will, sooner or later. Just a matter of time. It was a sadness born from grief. I almost got it, too."

"What grief?" he asked absentmindedly.

I told him the truth again. "Our daughter, Clare. She was thirteen, and he never saw her again."

"Running from home, eh?" he nodded. "I did that when I was a teenager, too. Didn't think my parents cared as much as you do. She'll probably come back when she needs food and supplies. All teenagers do that."

I made a noise suggesting that I heard what he said, and the conversation soon ended in the howling of winds.

* * * * *

The next morning we started off again, walking into the dense mist. I had to wipe my eyes every half an hour to get rid of the droplets of icy water collecting inside my lashes. They ran down my face like tears. The sky was a clear cerulean. The path trotted by goats came to an end, so we had to climb up the rocky landscape with bare hands and the rope Hansen brought. Some of the rocks were sharp like protruding onyx knives, and I carefully avoided them. Another advantage of being small is that if you're nimble enough, you can go where others can't. Hansen didn't mind the blade-like rocks for they break and shatter on his armor like glass thrown towards a brick wall.

We arrived at the entrance of the Cave, just in the afternoon.

"That's it?" I asked.

It looked the same as any other cave I've seen, perhaps even more ordinary than some I've seen, made with stormy gray rocks and nothing more. No torches on the walls, no crystals growing from the rocks, no ancient runes running along the floors, no eerie smoke coming from inside, and no unspeakable sense of dread filling the air around its presence.

"What, you expect to see guards?" Hansen barked a laugh.

"Perhaps," I replied, "it's a cave full of gold."

He spat on the ground. "Every villager here knows how to get here. They're just too wise to do it. I didn't think there really was a curse. I took gold from the Cave."

"And you've used that gold to buy a large house, live a rich life, and to marry your wife."

Beams of dusk danced across his scarred, wolfish face in fleeting shades of pink and gold. "True. And whatever I bought with that gold cannot make me happy. I feel nothing when I kiss my wife. Life in that house is just a bit better than that around the borders as a rogue."

There was silence, pierced only by the winds soaring around us, circling the top of Mount Mirk like a mother looking for her lost daughter. Patches of purple and orange light dappled upon me as I broke the silence. "Rogue life must be tough."

"You don't know the half of it," he sneered.

I shrugged, and felt my mist-damped hair sliding across my shoulder blades in little tendrils. "You ever killed anyone?"

"Of course. I was a rogue."

"What about women? Have you ever killed any women, Randy Hansen?" I asked in a flat tone.

"No," he said, almost on reflex. "No true man would kill women. I haven't."

"I heard it was a girl," I said.

I waited.

He picked out the words after a long silence rang between us. "I didn't kill that girl. I was a rogue, looking for a valuable procession to claim. I saw her, herding sheep. Ones with fur the color of soft snowfall, the best kind in the Highlands. She yelled at me, saying the sheep belonged to her family. She was quite pretty, but still too young for me… Anyway, I held a dagger to her throat to shut her up."

"Then?"

"I dragged her behind a cluster of dead trees and tied her there with her hair. I took the sheep. Maybe I did something wrong."

" 'Maybe'?"

"I didn't kill her," he said. "They probably wouldn't find her since the place was deserted, but I didn't kill her. I don't kill women. Or girls."

I blinked hard, and the image that had burnt itself into my eyelids appeared before me once again, hauntingly detailed as always. Highland summers were dry and windy, with dead wood and crisp leaves, things to burn with the slightest sparks of flame. It was the middle of June when I found her, the dead leaves and twigs that had concealed her from the rest of us burnt away by forest fire. I ran through smoke so thick they clung to the insides of my lungs the way a small child clings to her mother. I pushed burning trunks out of the way and heard the fibers rip. The forest fire burnt down even the oldest meadows that had been there longer than history and left blackened ashes in its wake.

I found her hanging, by blackened, twisted bones, to the half-burnt trunk of a tree. Flesh was burnt apart to the point that they hardened and cracked apart like broken clay, exposing her insides. Thin streaks of gray smoke rose from the remaining, once auburn hair as a soft rain of black ashes fell from the skeleton's empty sockets.

* * * * *

I walked into the cave without glancing back.

The cave was much deeper than it seemed, and shadows danced across walls as I walked. My vision in the dark was better than most people. I trained myself after what happened that day. Swordsmanship, martial arts, senses, and will power. I was a petite woman, with hands no bigger than a child's, but I could make these hands take life the way children pluck wool from bushes. And I would.

I saw no gold. The space around me was dark and empty, my footsteps echoing into a long distance away and back, but of course I saw no gold. The Cave does not present gold to people.

*It presents what you desire.* A voice whispered, the sound slithering leisurely around me. *And you don't want gold, unlike the others I've seen. You want revenge.*

"He killed my daughter," I said.

*Aye,* said the voice. *And you are fully prepared to take his life for it. Name them, the things you desire. Tell me what it is you long for, and I shall provide.*

I thought of afternoon walks by grassy hillsides, thought of the scent of strawberry jam in our warm kitchen, thought of charred, ruined skin and my daughter's broken form, and thought of Clare dancing to the music in the wind, her skirt fluttering around her ankles, hair that looked exactly like mine lit by sunlight, her smile tarnishing the rest of the world.

"I want a weapon. Give me a blade of any kind, and I'll do it," I told the Cave.

*Why still ask for a blade,* asked the voice, *when you've already brought your own knife, hidden in the sleeve of your cloth?*

"An ordinary blade will not pierce his armor," I said with a dead kind of calm that surprised even myself. "Any mortal weapon breaks when they but touch the surface of his armor. I've seen how it works. It covers all vulnerable spots."

The voice made a low hissing which I realized was its way of laughing. *Good,* it said. *You are observing and calculating. It means you are ready. Reach out your hand, and you shall find your blade.*

I reached blindly into the nothingness of the Cave, and vaguely saw the calluses all over my palm and fingertips from the whole two years of training I did, driven by hatred and a broken heart. I was a mother who loved her daughter. Now I am more than that.

Out from the darkness and the shadows I pulled a dagger with a blade the color of ink, the hilt of it as cold as death.

The voice spoke again, *The rogue would be waiting outside, waiting for you to return with gold. He plans to kill you when you do so. And so you must not hesitate.*

"I know," I said softly, my fingers dancing across the icy hilt of the dagger. I sent the blade spinning in a whooshing circle around my wrist, flung it upwards so high it disappeared from view, then caught it with a snap of two fingers and slashed at the air before me. I heard wind ripping as I sliced it in half neatly, then straightened as if nothing happened.

*You want your revenge,* asked the voice, its tone almost curious, *even if there is no happiness within to be earned? People get no pleasure from me. You know the rule.*

I didn't answer. I wanted no happiness as I deserved none after failing to find her when she needed me. I only wanted him dead, to give my daughter peace in the other world. And I was ready.

\* \* \* \* \*

It was hard to tell how much time passed while I was in the Cave. A slightly unsettling fact, for my sense of time had become very sharp from counting the days I've thrived without my family. I guess it didn't matter then. Not anymore.

It was midnight when I emerged from the Cave, my cloak and hair soaked with lingering shadows. Hansen sat a small distance away from the entrance of the Cave, his squared jaw propped against the leather hilt of his sword. His blood-shot eyes followed me as I walked inside the shadows cast by the rocky landscape, the dagger hidden out of view beneath my cloak. Heavy wind swirled around us, as the starless night sky stayed silent in a curtain of foggy blue and black. I saw a piece of waning moon, shining above us with a ghostly glow like an executioner's blade.

"What took you so long?" Hansen grumbled as he got to his feet, and I could see the hints of tension in his right hand that held his sword. I said nothing. There wasn't a need to. I walked around the small clearing we made camp in, concealing myself in the shadows. It was another advantage of being petite. I could hide easily. Hansen squinted into the dark with an exasperated look. And then I struck.

With one clean swipe of my blade I cut at his wrist before nailing it with the hilt of my weapon and sent his sword flying across the clearing. It landed with a metallic clang at the edge of the cliff. He swore and grabbed at me, but I backed away faster than his movement, poising the dagger in front of me.

We stared at each other from either side of our makeshift campsite, Hansen clutching his injured hand with his good one. "What the hell is the meaning of this?"

I answered him by skipping toward the edge of the clearing, then sent his sword clattering down the side of Mount Mirk with a kick.

"What was that for?" Hansen snarled. "If I wanted to kill you with my sword, I would've GODDAMN DONE IT on the way. I had tons of chances."

"But I didn't have gold with me then," I said with the utmost calm. "A man with gold is always in danger, you said. Or are you perhaps too thick to recall?"

He stared at me, yet I found nothing terrifying about the supposedly threatening act. We started walking around the clearing in cautious circles, studying each other, him grinding his teeth and my gaze cold. Thin streaks of moonbeams fell upon our backs like the gaze of an audience.

Randy Hansen was a tall, muscular, fully-grown man. I was out for blood. Only one of us would walk away alive from this.

"Why didn't you bring back gold?" he demanded, picking a piece of stone the size of a ram's horn from the ground.

"Because I don't want any," I said coldly, then continued on with a softer tone of voice. "All the villagers who live at the foot of this mountain know the path towards that cave. Tell me, Randy Hansen, why do you think it had to be you whom I made my guide? You, a former rogue."

His jawline tightened, eyeing me up and down, his voice a low growl. "I have no idea what the HELL you're talking about!"

"Clare," I said. The name burnt the insides of my throat, but my hands were steady as I pointed the tip of the dagger at him. "The girl you murdered. Her name was Clare. She was thirteen and wanted to be a dancer."

I wasn't sure if he heard me, or if he even cared. Hansen's head jerked once as the only response, then came charging towards me with the stone. He couldn't attack me the way he would an opponent around average adult height, and made the mistake I was waiting for him to make by bending lower to strike at me. I sidestepped his attack and thrust the dagger upwards with both arms, knowing exactly where I was aiming for. I heard a grunt, then pushed him with all my body weight. Hansen staggered backwards, cursing as blood oozed from the deep stab on his shoulder blade. Red seeped through his shirt from the gash on his armor, which he examined with an expression of disbelief and fear.

His face paled. "My arm. I can't move it."

"I expect so," I said softly, sliding a digit down the back of my blade, the blood-stained metal leaving a gentle coldness upon the calluses on my fingertip, like the touch of a ghost child's hand. As I took a step forward, he took a step back. I locked eyes with Randy Hansen, saw the frustration and the fear in his wolfish features, saw moonlight soaking into the fabric of his clothes along with the blood, throwing a thin sheen of glittery silver atop the crimson. I saw the man who killed the love of my life, and saw the man who I would kill with these very hands.

*****

I hung him, like a puppet with its strings cut, on the branches of an old dead tree. Hansen stared at me, and hissed through gritted teeth as a trail of blood dripped continuously from the corner of his mouth.

"I should've known. You have the same hair as that girl," he said.

His coarse language polluted the air around us as the night slowly faded into the light. I wouldn't kill him directly, as he didn't my daughter. I left the dagger in the earth just a few steps away from the tree, precisely just out of his reach when he tried his hardest to stretch his still functional arm. That done, I turned, and with the golden sunrise upon my hair the same color as hers, I walked away.

Clare, your mother loves you. Always.

# El Segundo, California
## by Fin Ryals

As a child, my favorite summertime souvenir was
Not seashells or sand crabs but
The tar that stuck to my salty feet
Like a sailor's tattoos
And I'd dance upon the web-like shadow of
The water treatment plant
That I mistook as part of the refinery
In hopes of staining myself permanently

My efforts were no match for my mother who
Armed with a rusty can of acetone and a blue
Hand towel battle-scarred and fossilized from
Past summer ventures lifted my feet against my
Will and scrubbed away tar pits with the sharpness of
A stingray's barb my throat filled with fumes from the
Chemical concoction used to besmirch the beach's mark on me and
I'd cry not from the galvanic aroma of the acetone
But from my taunting, freshly cleaned flesh that
Lingered on where the tar once did

# Sea Goddess
## by Justin Ratcliff

As your red hair wraps around my stilled heart
Your love vein begins its rapid resuscitation
I open my pitch black eyes to a gleaming silhouette
Blinding beam of passion transferred through your soul's window

Soft warm hand on my broad chest
Lost...oh so pleasantly lost in thee
The all encompassing fixation of us
Zeroed into a spiral of endless possibility

Your love is the first storm I willingly traverse
The high waves, still waters, or dark depths
Every and all aspects give life to my love
You boundless seas will be my Atlantis

# A Seaworthy Soul
## by Nicholas Yandell

We should fear the ocean.

Something we know without being told.

Enter extremity:

A shifting mass
Easily knocking us to the sand
With such obvious
Unrestrainable
Power.

I almost died in the ocean once
                        But breath broke through
                                    The suffering void
                          And aspiring skin
            Touched the shore again.

Since that haunted evening
The sea and I
Have a complicated relationship.

                I can't help the rush of memories
                        The flash of dark places
                                The terror-chilled sensations
                        Always accompanying
            Any marine interaction.

But after nearing demise
            A perplexing bond emerged
                                Between me
                And my would-be
       Liquid
   Assassin.

Some unseen part
　　　　I left out there
　　　　　　　　　　Replaced
　　　　　　　With insatiable
　　　Salt water
Desire.

When reunited with the sea
　　　　　I take the opportunity
　　　　　　　　　　　To throw out my arms
　　　　　　　　　　　　　　Dash to the waves
　　　　　　　　　　　　And submerge
　　　　　　　　Letting its salty fingers
　　　Touch every part of me.

Is this literal immersion therapy?

Some strange pilgrimage
　　　　　To near-death trauma?

　　　　　　　　Some twisted
　　　　　　　　　　　　Nautical
　　　　　　　　　　　　　　　Codependency?
　　　　　　　　　　　　　　　Or maybe the sea
　　　　　　　　　　　　　Enticing me
　　　　　　　Is just a closeted
　　　　　*L'appel du vide?*

Whether I have the words
　　　　To describe what it is
　　　　　　　Really doesn't matter.

　　　　　　　　　When breaking the surface
　　　　　　　And gulping relief
I can't help but feel renewed.

　　　　　　　　　　　　　A change of the winds
　　　　　　　　　　　A shift in perception
　　　　　　　　　Are welcome detours,
　　　　　　I undoubtedly needed.

　　　　　And perhaps the threat
　　　　　　　　Of losing one's breath

Will always be motivation
To live more vibrantly.

But in this fog of unknowns
Swayed by storms of doubt
And tides of forgetfulness
What still rises to certainty
Is the clear emergence
Of my seaworthy soul
And that's truly something
I thank the waves for.

# Cora Visits the Seaweed Kingdom
## by Kate Falvey

*In the darkness,*
*women and children*
*are wading in the water.*

I. Cebu, Visayan Sea

When the imagination fails
to discover a girl, Magdalena,
scanning the tie lines
for clumps of swaying guso,
the harvesting of which will
school her into lifting on more
distant, choppy, speculative seas.


II. Gorumna, Droim Quay, Ceantar na nOileán

Bríd Ní Mháille keened into
the waters in Boston Harbor and her dirge

reached back to Connacht where her brothers
swirled like carageen in the currents,

their currach capsized by a mystery
that's been guarded this hundred sixty years.

Rammed, they say,
but what was it that rammed?

Peader, Sean, and Briddy's fair, sweet Michael
rowed from quay to wilder seas to fish.

Martin had drowned before them so perhaps, they say,
'twas his envious ghost dragged his own kin down.

Some blame a ruthless, bitter sidhe from Tir fo Thuinn,

the land beneath the waves, who felt the pulse and glide

and earthy muscle of the crew and filled their boat with
tugging rage and anguish of ancient heavy hearts sinking.
*In the water,*
*women and children*
*are wading in the darkness.*


III. Cobscook Bay, Moose Island, Maine

The season for harvesting alaria esculenta brings
wistful ecotourists wishing they, too, had dug in

years ago and worked the seabed, surf, and rocky
tidelines, gathering and drying, snipping the tender

bits into a self-sufficiency of miso soup and salad,
mulch, and anti-aging face creams.

And, as she presses her slick boot-heel into the foggy
roughness of the sand and settles on a flattish gabbro

outcrop in the chill of early May to stare longingly
into the pool where sea stars, limpets, whelks, and

winkles, green crab, barnacles, blue muscles, snails
drift and burrow in a small enormity of tidal forest,

she sways, leaning into the algae and sea-greenery,
with a long-ago memory of spines of winged kelp

thick against the green luminosity
of her salt-glazed cheek.

*Her wet black hair is lost at sea.*

She scries the tidal current in the knee-deep pool
and sees small feet among the grabbling crustaceans,

flimsy and whelming, and sometimes carnivorous.
There is diaphanous blood and crushed spangles of bone

meal for the mollusks,
a transparency of stone.


IV.

She is surrounded by water
and mischance
but she wades in.
Fish, plainly speaking.
She was happy then.

# Bearings
## by Alex Richardson

I'm here to fetch things that float up,
Devoted to the murk of ocean,

No hint whatever it is
A few feet below,

Where iridescence waves
Before vanishing.

I come to this dock
Each morning

And imagine
A flounder, the wise seer,

Gazing from his abyss
Through tricks of light

At the stranger craning his neck
In a separate heaven.

# I Know That If I Shrunk Down To Three Inches Tall My Cat

by Cecily Cecil

would eat me without a thought because
        instinct is like that. I also know that she
                cherishes me the way a child cherishes

his first word, or the way his mother does. But
        loyalty is the victim of nature, and isn't
                that a beautiful excuse for everything

we've ever done? When I didn't call you for
        over a year, I told myself that was ok because
                it's in my nature not to pick up the phone

when all I want is to be alone and, hey,
        introverts are just like that, like cats
                basking in the sun and then suddenly

chasing their shadows or the light reflecting
        from a cell phone because they have no choice
                against DNA. But now I can't call you because

sometime between daydreaming a three-inch
        stature and being devoured by my cat, I forgot
                to miss you, and you fell asleep for the last time.

# Town of Dust
## by Audra Burwell

Vague images sway through my skull,
Sloshing under the dented cranial dome,
Like a liquid motherboard, uprooting strands
Of a dream, I thought had been long forgotten.

As the motion-picture reel plays, I step inside
Myself, not far enough to become lost in the
World of cracked screens and wavering signals,
But close enough to taste the bitterness of memory.

A ghost town veiled in clouds of dust and antiquity
Emerges, ramshackle buildings roofed in wooden
Shingles, brass hitching posts lining cobbled streets,
White linen fluttering from splintered fence posts.

Solitude settles over the abandoned village,
Temperature rising, the desert wind growing hotter
And more abrasive as it pelts my sweat-soaked
Neck with grains of stinging sand and heated mire.

Tumbleweeds roll across my path, bristling with their
Own sense of revulsion as I enter a boarded-up saloon,
My leather boots whispering as they scuff the whisky-
Stained floor, my thighs clad in faded black denim.

I look down at a body that no longer exists, a vessel
Of youth and innocence, thirteen years old again, a
Shock that warps reality, forcing me to question
Whether this omen links to the past or the future.

The air wavers, rippling like a decanter of water
Disturbed by exterior forces, the edges of the room
Blurring and receding as the scene shifts, radio static
Blaring in my ears, my only tether to the present.

Another layer of the dream unfurls, dragging my body
With it, folding and crunching my bones so they will fit,
Before propelling me through the glass dome of the
TV, and depositing me in front of my rewritten future.

# A Candle in the Window
## by Marie Dolores

Damask curtains at the top of the stairs have been tied back. The candle will burn for hours on the windowsill while I sleep. A dream told me he would come, but I need to let him know where to find me. Three weeks have passed and no one has appeared; but I can't give up. Not yet. Not while I'm still having the same dream each night.

A red taper stands tall in the old fashioned brass chamberstick. In this modern world of electric lighting it's not meant to literally light the way. It's a beacon, a symbol that I'm ready. It didn't have to be a taper, it could have been a votive or even a tea light, but this is my interpretation.

My friend Ruth brought the candles with my weekly groceries. She said the color was festive. I wonder what she'd think if I told her what they're for. She's the only one that comes anymore. The rest have run out of ways to say they're sorry for what I'm going through. I don't blame them. They're busy looking forward, while I spend too much time looking back.

I never married. It wasn't a conscious decision; it just never happened. Either our puzzle pieces couldn't connect at all, or appeared to fit, but there were gaps wide enough for one of us to slip through. I had work, the tennis club, concerts and art galleries. Time drifted, something shifted, and now it's just memories. At least I have those.

Lighting the wick signals the start of my bedtime ritual. Once it's safely in place, I shuffle off to the bathroom to wash my face and brush my teeth. It takes a while for the warm water to reach the upper rooms, and although I hate the waste, I can't bear a cold assault on my face. Pressing the thick, soft towel firmly onto my cheeks and forehead, I wait for the shudder to pass. The toothpaste tastes like dust as I swirl the brush over my teeth. Come to think of it, most things taste like dust, anymore.

Cavities are the least of my worries, I think, as I spit the gritty residue into the sink.

My left hand shakes as I reach for the bottle in the center of the counter. It will stop the trembling, at least temporarily, and blot out the pain that has been growing steadily since the last dose. White for pain and yellow to help me sleep. I'm up to six of the white ones a day – the pain worsening with each setting of the sun. My eyes squeeze shut and one hand grips the countertop as the oblong pills slip awkwardly down my throat. If only he would come soon.

After undressing, muscles protesting each movement, I slip the silky nightgown over my head. It's one of my remaining indulgences; I never could abide flannel. Then I totter over to the commode. 'Almost there; wash your hands and the bed is yours,' I coax myself as I finish the last of the routine.

A soft mattress cradles my body as I push and pull the pillows into a comfortable position. The drugs will kick in soon, providing blissful relief, however short-lived. Glancing once more through the doorway to the window and candle, I close my eyes and wait for release.

The dream starts the same as it has for weeks. A voice in the mist telling me to light a candle each night and soon he will come to take away the pain. It follows the normal progression until the mist starts to lift – something that had never happened before.

Slowly, the disappearing fog reveals shiny black oxfords. Dark grey pinstripe trousers just brush the top of the laces as the mist continues to rise. A double set of pewter buttons hold the suit coat securely in place. His hands are at his sides, relaxed and well groomed. I admire his sturdy build as his face comes into focus. There is no beard, his head is covered in wavy black hair; but it's his smile and shining hazel eyes that make me hold my breath. More handsome than I expected. Warmth I haven't felt in years forms in my cheeks as my lips curve to smile shyly back.

"It's time," he says, still smiling. His right arm has risen and is held out towards me.

Throwing back the covers, I swing my feet over the edge of the bed then push myself into a standing position, shivering as my feet land on cold oak floorboards.

I hesitate. This isn't exactly what I'd been expecting. Was I still in my dream or was this real? Leaning to glance past his shoulder, I notice the candle still burns in the window, though half its original size.

"It's all right," he says, his voice calm and reassuring. "I've come to take care of you; just as promised. Take my hand and the pain will be gone forever."

"Forever?" I hear myself echo.

"No more pain and suffering, Amelia, I promise."

"Who are you?" Did it really matter? A twinge in my arm when I pushed myself out of bed accompanied the dull ache in my abdomen. It never fully went away anymore. Cancer is a terrible disease – eating its way through the body, devouring each healthy cell from the inside out. I was tired of the pain, so very tired of the pain. "No more suffering?"

"No more suffering," he replies, deep compassion flows from his eyes, wrapping me in a cloak of warmth in the chilly room. He takes a step forward, as I place a hand on the bed to steady myself while a wave of torment rattles through my weakened body.

"It's time," I decide.

"It's time," he assures me.

As I reach out, ready, now, to grasp his still outstretched hand, the light from the candle intensifies, filling the outer room with a warm, soft glow. As my fingers brush his, the pain vanishes. I'd forgotten what it felt like to not be in constant discomfort. No more abdominal pain, no more aches in my back, arms, or legs – gone as if they had never been there. Tears blur my vision at the overwhelming relief.

I glance up with childlike wonder and his own smile grows as his hand closes around mine. The candle flickers bright one more time; then goes out.

# Cum mortuis in lingua viva - A handover in letters. A collage.
by Lars Straehler-Pohl

January 19

Dear unknown sleepless friend,

Truly it is late at night. It becomes more and more difficult to dive into sleep, to find a way to slip into your dreams. Indeed— you would have swum out hours ago to reach the shore again in time. The ascending dawn makes the distance even longer, the water even colder, the heart beat faster.

We are miles, possibly years, apart from each other. I can only help from a distance. The best I can do for you right now is to hand you a bundle of letters. Letters from people who never met and yet still have answers for each other. Separated by centuries, as we now are separated, these human beings are connected by the lines they wrote.

Dear sleepless friend, letters are the quiet expansion of the short lifetime we are given. A gift from those in former times, echoes of past despairs and hopes. Don´t take them as monuments, don´t remain in reverence. Play with them. Treat them as an invitation to a relationship.

In some moments you might be too tired to form your thoughts, in the no man's land between sluggish wakefulness and sleeplessness. And sometimes you might be even too tired to find your own words. Do not worry. When this happens, let us start a kind of game. Take the letters I send you and pick some lines from them that seem most fitting to you in that moment. Send them back to me and I will answer you in the same manner. Send them whenever a silent voice from the outside is needed. No matter whether it is hours, days or years from now on. I will answer, we will answer. Dear friend, sleep well.

Yours, Paul

\*\*\*

February 1 / 12:52 a.m.

**The Insomniac** ...what a time your letters take to come! You can't think what a difference it makes when they bring in a blue envelope.¹ I've had to retire to bed with the usual old pain.²

12:58 a.m.

**Paul** This news that I hear just now, is very upsetting to me – all the more as I assumed from your last letter that you were, thank God, quite well. – But now I hear that you are truly ill!³

1:24 a.m.

**The Insomniac** I thank you for this new evidence of your concern for me, all the more because I am so little deserving of it with you.⁴ I was sick and still am today, my stomach is acting up⁵ ...as if my stomach were a person and wanted to cry.⁶ Lately, for example, a wave of unrest has swept over me once more, insomnia, suffering from the slightest noise and they arise literally out of the air.⁷ My sense of hearing has become a thousand times sharper and yet that much more uncertain. If I run my finger over a sheet, I no longer can say for certain whether or not I am hearing a mouse. But the mice are not fantasies, as the cat comes in to me skinny in the evening and is carried out fat in the morning.⁸

1:09 a.m.

**Paul** I need not tell you, at least I hope so, how eagerly I await some comforting news from you—although it's become my habit to always imagine the worst of everything.⁹

                                                                                    1:37 a.m.

**The Insomniac** I myself am untouched and my hair is no whiter than yesterday, but it was the horror of the world. What a terrible, dumbly raucous folk they are[10]...and now I see a fresh hole next to the door. So mice here, too. And the cat is unwell today, throwing up constantly.[11]

But what are you missing?[12]

                                                                                    1:39 a.m.

**Paul** I believe I drank too much wine last night.[13] I slept quite well, with only the mice as my good and virtuous company—I had a right proper discussion with them.[14]

                                                                                    1:42 a.m.

**The Insomniac** You think you have nothing against mice? Of course, and you have nothing against cannibals, either, but when they crawl out from under all the boxes at night and bare their teeth, you won't like them anymore. What I feel with mice is simply anxiety. To figure out where it comes from is a matter for the psychoanalysts, not me.[15] I don't believe that there is a writer's or musician's sleep that will hold out against them, and no corresponding heart that wouldn't overflow, not really with fear, but with disgust and sadness. But even this is only in jest, because I haven't heard anything suspicious for a long time, thanks to the cat...[16]

                                                                                    1:59 a.m.

**Paul** Here's my brain now quite bright, but purely critical. It can read; it can understand.[17] I could also put myself to the test in my own mouse hole. And this is it: a fear of utter loneliness.[18] Hey, do you understand the feeling that one must bear, pulling a yellow mail coach full of sleeping people alone through the long night?[19]

2:02 a.m.

**The Insomniac** I have seen much that you have written.[20]

2:14 a.m.

**Paul** Yes, I do write damned well sometimes, but not these last days.[21]

Here is another selfish invalid's bulletin, but I like to write to you, and you won't mind it all being about myself[22]...thus you know how I feel about life, out there, stumbling along over the cobblestones, like the poor mail coach.[23] But what about loneliness? Basically, loneliness is my only aim, my greatest lure, my possibility, and, assuming that one can speak at all of having 'arranged' one's own life, it was always with a view to the fact that loneliness is a comfortable part of it. And yet there is the fear of that which I love so much. It is significant, by the way, that I feel so comfortable in empty apartments—not in completely empty ones, but in those that are full of memories of all the people and prepared for further life, apartments with furnished matrimonial bedrooms, children's rooms, kitchens; apartments into which the early morning mail for others is dropped in, where newspapers for others are left at the door. But the real inhabitant must never show up, as happened to me the other day—that I find terribly disturbing. Well, that's the story of the 'breakdowns'.[24]

2:27 a.m.

**The Insomniac** I hope and pray that as I write this you are feeling better; but if contrary to all assumptions, this is not so, I ask you not to conceal it from me, but to write to me, or have someone write, the plain truth, so that I can be in your arms as quickly as is humanly possible.[25]

2:29 a.m.

**Paul** I ride my motorcycle a lot, I swim a lot, I lie naked in the grass by the pond for long periods.²⁶

2:31 a.m.

**The Insomniac** By the way, I'm not giving up hope for you at all, I must tell you that. You are easily despaired, but also easily happy, keep this in mind when you are in despair. Safeguard your health for better times to come. What you are going through seems bad enough, but don't aggravate it by damaging your health.²⁷

2:35 a.m.

**Paul** Have you ever been as weary of someone as you are of me just now?²⁸

2:36 a.m.

**The Insomniac** So, weary, but obedient and grateful: I thank you. Everything is fine now, isn't it? And since it's winter, we're sitting—it's the truth—in a room, except that the walls behind where each of us is sitting are a bit far apart, but that's merely a bit odd and doesn't have to be.²⁹

3:09 a.m.

**Paul** Be well. You've helped me a lot in the last few days.³⁰ Letters can delight me, move me, evoke admiration in me, but they used to mean much more to me, too much, for them to be an essential form of life for me now. I have not been deceived by letters, but I have fooled myself through letters, literally warming myself for years in advance from the warmth they yielded when the whole heap of letters finally went into the fire...³¹

3:11 a.m.

**The Insomniac** Thunder is good, thunder is impressive; but it is the lightning that does the work.³² Time to go to sleep.³³

3:14 a.m.

**Paul** I never go to bed without reflecting on the possibility that (young as I am) there might not be another day. And yet no one who knows me can say that I'm sullen or sad to be around. And for this felicitousness I give thanks every day and wish the same with all my heart for my fellow human creatures.³⁴ But enough – don't die –³⁵

3:43 a.m.

**The Insomniac** The truth is, I have a great deal to do; and I have made up my mind not to die till it is done.³⁶ Maybe I'll become a village fool; the current one that I saw today appears to be living in a neighboring village and is rather old.³⁷ Your letter is here, I step into it like someone who, weary of the field paths, is now entering the woods. I'll lose my bearings, but am not afraid. If only every day could end like this.³⁸

With warmest regards, yours sincerely, Franz³⁹

\*\*\*

*Epilogue*

11:22 a.m.

**Franz** Early today, between Jan. 31st and Feb. 1st, I woke up around five o'clock and heard you calling 'Franz' outside the room door, gently, yet I heard it clearly. I answered immediately, but there was nothing more. What did you want?⁴⁰

11:24 a.m.

**Paul** You will not suspect me of affectation, dear friend, or of any unworthy passion for being mysterious, merely because I find it impossible to tell you now—in a letter—what that one question was.⁴¹

11:33 a.m.

**Franz** What are you carrying so carefully in that box? A treasure perhaps, or a proclamation, right? Well, open it up, we could use both![42]

11:40 a.m.

**Paul** Nothing but hope for a better state of affairs.[43] I feel that you cannot misunderstand me.[44]

[1] Virginia Woolf, 52 Tavistock Square, February 4, 1929.
[2] Virginia Woolf, Monk's House, August 12, 1929.
[3] Wolfgang Amadeus Mozart, April 4, 1787.
[4] Ludwig van Beethoven, Vienna, November 16, 1801.
[5] Franz Kafka, Prague, January 31, 1916 [1917].
[6] Franz Kafka, Prague, June 19, 1909.
[7] Franz Kafka, Matliary, May 1921.
[8] Franz Kafka, Zürau, November 24, 1917.
[9] Wolfgang Amadeus Mozart, April 4, 1787.
[10] Franz Kafka, Mid-November 1917.
[11] Franz Kafka, Zürau, November 24, 1917.
[12] Franz Kafka, Jungborn, December 17, 1912.
[13] Jane Austen, Steventon, November 20, 1800.
[14] Wolfgang Amadeus Mozart, June 25, 1791.
[15] Franz Kafka, Zürau, Early December, 1917.
[16] Franz Kafka, Zürau, Mid-December 1917.
[17] Virginia Woolf, June 5, 1927.
[18] Franz Kafka, postmarked November 9, 1922.
[19] Franz Kafka, September 6, 1903.
[20] Edgar Allan. Poe, May 19, 1848.
[21] Virginia Woolf, 52 Tavistock Square, June 18, 1926.
[22] Virginia Woolf, 52 Tavistock Square, January 29, 1929.
[23] Franz Kafka, Prague, August 24, 1902.
[24] Franz Kafka, Plana, postmarked September 11, 1922.
[25] Wolfgang Amadeus Mozart, April 4, 1787.
[26] Franz Kafka, Triesch, Middle of August, 1907.
[27] Franz Kafka, Prague, June/July 1914.
[28] Franz Kafka, Prague, February 4, 1902.
[29] Franz Kafka, Prague, November 1917.
[30] Franz Kafka, Spindlermühle, January 31, 1922.
[31] Franz Kafka, Prague, January, 1922.
[32] Mark. Twain, Redding, Connecticut, August 28, 1908.
[33] Mark Twain, Redding, Connecticut, 3:00 a.m., April 17, 1909.
[34] Wolfgang Amadeus Mozart, April 4, 1787.
[35] Virginia Woolf, Monk's House, December 25, 1938.
[36] Edgar Allan. Poe, New York City, December 30,1846.
[37] Franz Kafka, Zürau, September 22, 1917.
[38] Franz Kafka, Prague, Early October, 1907.
[39] Franz Kafka, Prague, June 5, 1913.
[40] Franz Kafka, 1921.
[41] Edgar Allan. Poe, New York City, May 19, 1848.
[42] Franz Kafka. Kafka, January 10, 1904.
[43] Ludwig van Beethoven, Vienna, November 16, 1801.
[44] Edgar Allan Poe, New York City, May 19, 1848.

# The Train
## by A.R. Bender

  I pulled aside tightly packed furniture items on the basement floor of my dimly-lit apartment storage area, searching for boxes containing some old family photos. At last, I found them and eventually the one box with the photos I'd been looking for. They all were taken about twenty years before when I was ten years old in the mid-1960s and when my mother took my sister, Aline, and I to visit my grandparents in München, Germany. I hadn't bothered to go through them in many years, but was driven down to these dark confines by a rather vivid dream I had about my grandmother that morning.

  They were all in black-and-white and brought back poignant memories of that summer. One picture showed me climbing an apple tree in my grandparent's yard, and another where I sat at the dinner table next to my uncles and grandfather. I chuckled at the photo of me in the driver's seat of my uncle's Mercedes sedan with my hands on the steering wheel, pretending to be driving and with such a wild and goofy grin. And most precious of all: the picture of me sitting in my grandmother's lap as she read a story from a book of fairy tales. I trudged up the stairs carrying the box, with the idea of putting the photos into an album.

  I stared into the murky gloom outside the kitchen window while waiting for the coffee to brew. The milky fog partially obscured the dark shapes of trees and buildings across the street, but the weather report said it was going to clear up later in the morning—another typical San Francisco day. Headlights from passing cars going up and down a steep Telegraph Hill street cast luminous beams into the haze. A lone, hunched figure shuffled along the sidewalk in front of my place, stopped for a moment as if lost, and continued walking into the mist.

  I turned on a classical music radio station, plopped down on the easy chair with the coffee, and thought more about the dream. It was similar to an experience I had many times that summer when we took train trips from a München suburb to the city. During these trips, I always sat in a window seat, so I could wave goodbye to grandmother as the train slowly pulled away from the station. Except in this dream, she was the one in the train waving goodbye to me from an open window.

A Gustav Mahler symphony played on the radio. Now more memories burst forth about my grandmother, or Oma, as Aline and I lovingly called her. The first thing I recalled were the times we walked together along the dirt roads of the rustic Obermenzing neighborhood in the mornings, passing by old houses with spacious yards sheltered by overgrown shrubs and trees—some with chickens, roosters, goats, or pigs—until we arrived at the station.

"Hey look, Oma!" I said, pointing up the tracks. "Here comes the train!"

"*Ja Ja*," she said. "*Ich sehe es*."

"Do you see it too, mom?" I asked.

"Yes, Bert, I do"

"So what?" Aline said. "It's just the same old train."

"I wish you could go with us this time," I said to Oma.

She shook her head, unable to understand, so mom translated my words to her. She nodded to me with a smile.

I stared at the dark shape of the locomotive as it rounded a curve in the distance. As it chugged closer, I got a strange sensation in the pit of my stomach, followed by an urge to jump down to the tracks, and then leap back up onto the platform just before it arrived. I couldn't take my eyes off the single glimmering headlight on the face of the engine, and felt lightheaded and dizzy as it rumbled closer. I only snapped out of it when the platform shook a little as the train shuddered to a stop.

Today we were going to the zoo. I jumped onto the train and sat down in one of the window seats facing the platform so

I could see Oma. We were off on another adventure! Even though we'd taken the same ride many times before, I always liked looking at the scenery as we passed the farms and countryside, the roads and autobahn, the villages and small towns, and then the larger towns, the outskirts of München, and finally the bustling railway station. There was always something new and different to see each time.

Aline and I waved to Oma from the window, and as soon as the train started to move out, I lifted up the window and waved to her again. She waved back with a warm smile, but with eyes that looked like she was crying. I watched her standing on the platform until the train rounded a bend, and she disappeared from view.

***

The sight and smell of all the food on the dinner table kicked in my appetite right away. As usual, my grandfather—or Opa, as Aline and I called him—sat at the head of the table. The main course was the oxtail soup full of the vegetables I helped Oma cut in the afternoon.

"*Mmm sehr gut, Mutti,*" Rolf remarked as he ate.

"*Ja. Das Fleisch ist zart,*" Wolfgang said.

"Mmm, you're right, uncle," I said. "The meat melts in my mouth."

"*Kleine Bertie half mir heute, Sie wissen,*" Oma said

"*Wirklich? Wie?*" Opapa asked

I remembered some German from the time I'd been there two summers before, and was beginning to understand the language better each day. "I cut some vegetables, that's all," I answered.

"Good for you," mom said.

"Probably the ugly mushy ones," Aline retorted.

"Oh shut up. I did better than you could."

"You two stop fighting or else no dessert," mom said.

"Bert speaks German very well," Rolf said to mom. He liked to speak English whenever he could. "Do you give him lessons?"

"No, he just listens well," she said.

"*Ja, er ist sehr klug,*" Opa said to Oma, "*wie ihre Bruder.*"

"*Hast du ein Bruder?*" I asked Oma.

"*Ja, aber ich habe noch vier Bruder.*"

"Wow, four brothers," I said. "*Hast du Schwesters?*"

"*Nein, ich habe keine Schwestern,*" she answered, with an amused smile.

"Oh, no sisters," I replied. "*Wo wohnst deine Bruders?*"

"*Drei in Stuttgart und eins in Ulm.*"

"We're going to visit them in Stuttgart soon," mom said.

"When?"

"*Wann haben Sie sagen, wir werden sie besuchen?*" Mom asked Oma.

"*Am nächsten Wochenende,*" Oma answered.

"Next weekend? Are we going by car or train?"

"By car," Wolfgang answered.

"Yeah! On the autobahn!"

\*\*\*

I was so glad to ride in Rolf's fast Mercedes with Wolfgang on the way to Stuttgart. The rest of the family rode in Opa's Opel sedan. We left in the morning and both cars rode together until they got on the autobahn, where Rolf sped off to pick up Gerhard, one of Oma's brothers, in Ulm

Rolf had taken me on short trips on the autobahn before, so I knew he liked to drive fast. I sat in the back seat and watched with glee as he passed almost every car on the autobahn. The only time he ducked into the right lane was when those funny-looking Porsches roared past us.

We arrived in Stuttgart in the early afternoon, but stayed in the residential areas. Rolf drove the car into a woodsy neighborhood with narrow streets and large and stately homes until he turned into a long driveway leading to one of those homes. After he parked, I got out and gazed at the house in awe, which looked as big as a castle.

A butler greeted us at the door, and we followed him through the house. All the rooms had rich woodwork and high beamed ceilings, with many old paintings of landscapes and portraits hanging on the walls. We emerged out of the house into a spacious backyard, interspersed with fruit trees and bordered by pruned shrubs, where groups of adults and children were socializing.

Most of the men stood in the partially shaded patio holding hefty mugs of beer. Rolf, Wolfgang, and Opa quickly headed toward them. Aline played on a swing with two other girls. A group of women sat on a table, including mom and Oma, in the shade under a large tree. On the other side of the yard, three boys about my age kicked a soccer ball around. I was about to join them until Oma waved and walked toward me, with a smile.

"*Ah es gibt sie Bertie,*" she said. "*Sie können sich meine Brüder jetzt—deine grosse Onkle.*"

She led me to a festive group of men. One of them broke off his conversation as we approached.

"*Auch Schwester,*" the man said to Oma. "*Wer ist dieser hübsche junge Mann mit ihnen?*"

"*Das ist Albert, Doris' Sohn,*" Oma answered, "*aber wir*

*nennen ihn Bert."*

"*Ach ja,*" the man said, with a broad grin "So you are my nephew. No, my grand-nephew."

"*Bert, das ist Eckhard, einer von meinen Brüdern,*" Oma said.

"*Gutentag, Eckhard,*" I said.

"*Gutentag, Bert. Sprechen Sie Deutsch?*"

"*Nur ein bischen.*"

"That is good enough," Eckhard said, with a hearty laugh.

Just then, a few other men gathered around Eckhard.

"These are my other brothers," Eckhard said, pointing to two men behind him, "Friedrich and Werner."

Both men nodded and gazed at me with fixed smiles.

"How do you like Germany?" Friedrich asked.

"I like Germany a lot," I answered. "This house too. It's so big."

"Yes, it has been in our family for many years," Eckhard said.

As we talked, I noticed one of the girls on the swing race across the yard and stand next to the men on the patio. She had blonde hair with long braids and stared intently at me as I spoke to my granduncles.

Just then, the butler came out to the patio and struck a triangular shaped bell with a metal rod.

"Ah, dinner is ready," Eckhard said. "I hope you are hungry."

The rest of the group followed Eckhard into the dining hall. On the way, the girl with braids ran up next to me.

"Hi, my name is Gretchen."

"I'm Bert."

"So, you're from the United States," she said

"Yeah. We're visiting our relatives in München. Are you from the U.S. too?"

"No. My family lives in Heidelberg."

"It's just that you speak English so well."

"My brother, Dieter, and I go to a school that teaches it. Let's talk more at the dinner table!"

The grownups all sat on the main table, while I sat in the middle of the smaller table with the other kids.

"Dieter, this is Bert, from the United States," she said to a boy across from us. "He's visiting relatives in München."

"Hi, Bert," Dieter said.

"I saw you playing soccer when I came here," I said.

"Soccer?" Dieter asked. "Oh, we call it fussball here."

"Football? We have another sport called football in the U.S."

"*Was sagts er?*" a boy next to Dieter asked.

Dieter muttered something in German to the boy, who responded with a laugh.

"Do you play soccer, Bert?" Dieter asked.

"I play with some boys in München."

"Good. You can join us next time you're here."

I spent the rest of the meal talking mostly to Gretchen while the others spoke amongst themselves in German. We feasted on roast chicken, potato pancakes with gravy and cabbage salad, and the two of us exchanged many little stories about life in each other's countries. I liked Gretchen. Even though she was a girl, she wasn't too girlish.

The next morning, I sat at the kitchen table with mom and Aline eating sausages and eggs and fresh bread, recalling the fun I had after the dinner with the other kids when they played in the vast cellar of the house. We followed secret tunnels down there by flashlight, which went on for long distances until metal gates prevented us from going any farther. Dieter said they were built a long time before and used as escape routes from invading enemies.

"What are you thinking about, Bert?" mom asked. "You're so quiet this morning."

"Oh, just all the fun I had here last night, especially in the basement. Do you think we can come here again?"

"We'll see."

I figured this meant a "no" because it was already the middle of August and we had to fly back to the States in a few weeks.

After breakfast, we all said goodbye to Eckhard and his brothers and headed outside toward our cars for the drive back to München. I glanced back to the house before I got back in the car, wishing we could stay in the house another day or two because I felt so good being inside it. I stood there for some time and couldn't take my eyes off it because I sensed if I did, something important would be lost to me forever.

"Let's go, Bert," Rolf said, from inside the Mercedes. "It's a long drive back."

Reluctantly, I got in the car and said little during the drive home, torn by confusing emotions I didn't understand. Maybe that's why I wanted to stay so much—we were leaving too soon!

\*\*\*

I tried to sleep but my mind was on other things, mostly

that we were going back home in a few days. In a way, I looked forward to the exciting plane trip, but the strongest feelings I had were ones of disappointment and sadness because of all the new friends I was going to leave behind, like Gretchen and Dieter. Another was Rovie, the boy next door. We explored the trails in the nearby woods, and played soccer together with the other neighborhood boys.

In fact, I was going to miss everything about Germany: the countryside and farms, the old and stately buildings in the city, the different kinds of cars, riding on the trains, and the way all the people talked and acted. Germany seemed like a place I felt more comfortable and at home in—so much more than in Seattle. Of course, I'd miss my uncles and Opa and Oma most of all!

Unable to sleep, I crept downstairs to see if anyone was still up. Wolfgang was reading a book by the fireplace and Oma sat on the other side of the room knitting a scarf.

"Bertie," she said. "*Was ist los? Kannst du nicht schlafen?*"

"*Nein Oma.*"

"*Hier kommen dann,*" she said, patting the chair, "*Ich lese Ihnen jetzt ein Buch.*"

I went to a nearby shelf and pulled out a familiar book: a hardbound collection of The Brothers Grimm Fairy Tales, which she'd read to me before.

"*Welche soll ich Ihnen vorlesen am Abend?*" she asked.

"*Ich weiß es nicht, Oma.*"

I sat down on the chair next to her and settled my head on her shoulder, soft as a pillow, after she opened the book. The pungent, musty aroma of her dress and the odor of her body transformed my imagination even deeper into the book. I'd seen and read many of the stories and their corresponding sketches before: The Frog Prince, Hansel and Gretel, The Enchanted Stag, Rapunzel, Little Red Riding Hood, The Clever Elf, Rumpelstiltskin, and others. Finally, she came upon a new story.

"*Ach, Der Verlorene Sohn,*" she said.

I could only understand a few words as she read to me in German, but it almost didn't matter. I gazed upon the sketches on each page and simply imagined what those words meant. In a way, that was almost better than reading the story in English. Soon, I started to nod off. I tried to stay awake in her comforting presence and in the fantasy world of the book; however, near the end of the story I drifted off to sleep.

The radio played a commercial, snapping me out of my reveries. I walked over to my book shelf and pulled out a copy of The Brothers Grimm Fairy Tales. I paged through it and came upon the story Oma last read to me, twenty years before: The Lost Son.

\*\*\*

The next Monday I was back at work on the newspaper, madly typing a column based on an extraction from the police blotter that came in on the wire over an hour late.

"Hey Bert!" Gus shouted from the other side of the office.

"Pick up line four. It's your mother from Seattle."

"Hello, mom?"

"Oh Bert," she said, in a distraught voice. "I'm sorry to call you at work, but it couldn't wait. And sometimes you don't answer your home phone."

"Is everything alright?"

"No. I just got a call from your Uncle Rolf in Germany. "My mother—your Oma," she said between sobs, "has passed away."

"Oh, no, I'm so sorry."

"He tried to call earlier but a storm disrupted the phone service there until today. Oh, I wish I wasn't so alone now. "

"Did you call Aline?"

"Yes, she's driving up from Portland today. That will help."

"I'll see if I can take a few days off to fly up there."

"That's so thoughtful but there won't be enough time. I have to catch a flight to Germany Wednesday for the funeral later this week. She sent a letter from her earlier this month," she said, breaking into sobs again. "Everything seemed alright—"

"You know, the other day—" I was going to tell her about the dream when I felt an odd tingly sensation in my gut. "When did it happen?"

"Just last week."

I was about to ask which day, but then it hit me. I knew exactly which day it happened.

# Into which what follows
## by Carolyn Adams

I live two months
each sleeping hour.

A set of fires burn
my night house.

I cover my eyes, slip slow
into cold
water.

Carrion birds gather
at the vigilant
edge of what I want when
I awaken.

It's never there, ever.

I age at the searing speed of light.

BIG FISH, LITTLE FISH - Carolyn Adams

# What do your dreams tell you?
## by Joan Mazza

Last night my ex-husband was with me,
very much alive and still my ally.
A young man has come to live with us

as helper, gardener, cleaner
and my ex accepts him without fear.
I've just adopted a black lab puppy

who gets along fine with my cats.
I walk home from Boca Raton to my
Ft. Lauderdale house without pain.

My dreams tell me what I want
to hear, that nothing is impossible,
especially everything that is.

# DEEP
# DOVE
# STOCK
# PRE

# Westerns

# Equus
## by Audra Burwell

Muscles churning, coiling, tightening, releasing,
Bunched beneath the rawhide saddle, slick with
Foam and sweat, a dirty brown lather frothing
At the shoulder, obscuring the flea-bitten gray
Coat wrapped around the powerful creature,
Whose magnificent galloping strides fly toward
A starlit horizon, soaked in plum and magenta.

Pounding hooves echo through the rain-washed canyon
Dripping in darkness and delirium, the sound cracking
Sharply against the rugged terrain, sun-baked and raw,
A visage hideous to the eye, but necessary for survival.
Veins pulse beneath russet legs, elegant and dainty on
The surface, but wrapped in sinewy tendons, sparks of
Fire igniting deep in the cells, a combustion of energy.

Chest heaving, puffs of chalky breath frost the sky,
Each one wavering, tendrils of steam curling around
Quivering lips slick with saliva, a beast of endurance,
Strength now waning, struggling against the restraints
Of mortal flesh, determined to faithfully serve a master
Whose bond runs deeper than the ancient bedrock
Underfoot, obscuring the soul of the Arabian desert.

Fists clenched, knuckles turning white, the hooded
Stranger leans forward in the saddle, one hand
Stroking the quivering neck of his steed, touch soft,
Soothing and gentle, allowing a warm stream of
Comfort to seep beneath its coat, an invisible thread
Of communication, telepathy, and clairvoyance, a quiet
Transference of energy blossoming between the two.

Fused as one mind, one body, rider and mount share
Their strength, each clinging to a stoicism quickly
Dimming, coalescing with the scarlet horizon, fleeting
Back to the foot of its creator. Their journey is at last
Nearing a close, each chapter of their past folded
Neatly like a pair of worn reins lying limp, waiting for
A new dawn to break, washing clean the endless night.

# I Will Never Be a Cowboy
## by BEE LB

*after Katrina Agbayani*

though i spent much of my life trying.
chased the barrels like i'd never known the rush of dizziness.
clutched the mane of a living thing like we were one and the same.
rode bareback in winter like my favorite childhood movie.
somewhere in a box left in my childhood home are all the ribbons
i might have won. somewhere in a landfill are all the ribbons i won
and lost.
somewhere in my mother's attic is a horse with a broken leg
porcelain showing through paint where it hit the ground
after leaving my father's violent hand. all it would take is a ring
of glue and care in setting to fix the figurine. i want *BEST IN SHOW*
for refusing to gentle my aunt's mustang colt.
*ALL AROUND COWBOY* for never knowing when to quit
or how to start. *BREAKAWAY ROPING* for perfect
timing without the cruelty of a fall. i want to bet
on the fat chance without pushing an animal
beyond its limits. i want the rush without the race.
the cowboy hat tucked down for that sheepish shot like all the
western boys
were the first to ever blush. i want to step to the second ring
of a rickety wood fence so i can lean over and kiss
another cowboy. i want the metal coil to brand
my hip, not the livestock. let's open up
all the pens, let the animals roam
free. let's pile the hay and pretend it's soft enough
to lay on. open the hatch in the hayloft and look out at the stars
even though you never see a cowboy
at night. let's pretend i'm the roughed up cowboy
and you're the buckle bunny and we're just gonna have a little fun.
we can pretend i've never heard the squeal
of a dying thing and you believe me when i tell you who i am
and who i'm not. let's pretend the heat of the sun is a stadium light
and the crow of the cock is the crowd cheering me on.
i want to touch the horns of a bull
and promise that i'll never make it
buck. let the fury steam
doused in cold water, touch nose to wet snout.

i've always been my worst animal. once, i kept a ring
between my two nostrils and promised
not to pull.

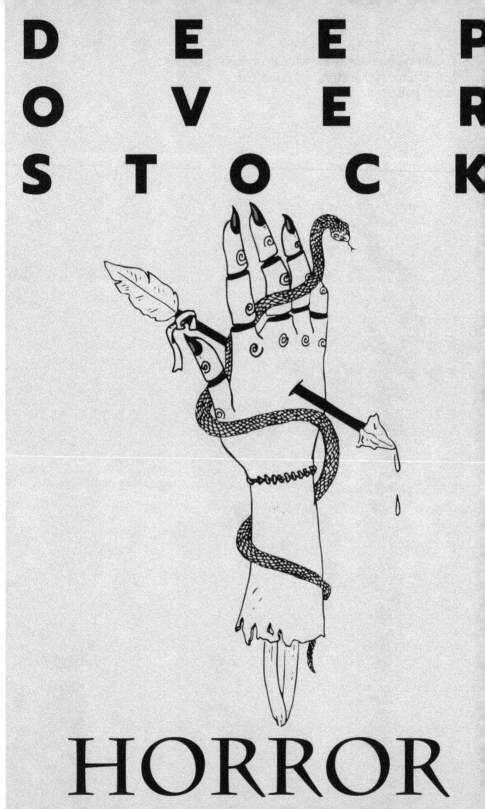

# Postcard From the Crypt

## by Deborah Coy

I hold your severed finger
in my hand.
I make it point
to the sky
to the place I'm sure you are.
I wish I had more of you
to cherish.

# The Color of Light
## by Ivan de Monbrison

The rain has come.
I no longer know what exactly the color of Light has behind its transparency.
I don't remember the sound of the wind blowing in my sleep.
There is a closed door somewhere that someone wants to open, but cannot.
All the noises are mixed up together, someone is shouting,
But it's not me anymore.
In my head, cut-off from my body and placed on the table, it's still not me watching you,
coming and walking to and fro into the Light, getting up to sleep, lying down to scream.
Behind your hand you hide your eyes from me, as if you wanted to avoid my thoughts.
And yet I don't think about nothing, as I've left my brain in the cupboard,
spinning in its box made of cardboard.
I take the letter paper that you had put in the desk drawer, and in spite of myself I start writing
Useless words that I don't even understand myself.
Tomorrow I will mail these words in envelopes to others who will probably not read them.
But my cut-off head has been hanging out on the table all this time,
since the other night,
and you, you,
Keep hiding your eyes with your hand, so that I can't see them,
nor even gouge them out.

# Цвет света

Пошел дождь.
Я больше не знаю, какого цвета свет за его прозрачностью.
Я больше не слышу звук ветра, дующего во сне.
Где-то есть закрытая дверь, которую кто-то хочет открыть,
но не может.
Все звуки смешиваются.
Кто-то кричит, но это не я.
В моей голове, оторванной от моего тела и лежала на
столе, это все еще не я смотрю на тебя,
уходит туда и сюда на свету, встаёшь чтобы спать и
ложишься чтобы кричит.
За своей рукой ты прячешь от меня глаза, как будто хочешь
избежать моих мыслей.
И все же я ни о чем не думаю,
потому что я оставил свой мозг в шкафу, который ходил по
кругу в своей картонной коробке.
Я беру бумагу для писем которые ты положила в ящик
стола, и моя рука несмотря на меня
начинает писать бесполезные слова, которых я не
понимаю.
Завтра я отправлю эти слова в конвертах на других,
которые не будут вероятно читать их.
А моя отрубленная голова все это время лежит на столе,
точно с вечера,
а ты, ты всегда
прячешь от меня глаза свои рукой, так что я не могу их
увидеть или даже вырвать.

# Tenuous Threads
## by Audra Burwell

We are parasites, bulbous bodies entangled,
Swarming atop nests of rotten flesh, fighting
And crowding on an already choked planet,
A hive mind of greed and gluttony, evil oozing
From our pores, sickly brown muck slicking
Our palms as we tear through dying matter.

Our bulging guts and sunken eyes scan for
Nourishment as we traverse the hollowed husk
We inhabit, moondust clinging to our scaled
Skin, bloody fingertips dripping black oil, a
Secretion of toxins pooling in the beds of our
Nails, black craters spreading and devouring.

Carnage has become our nature, bestial and
Savage, a dying race clinging to the tethers of
Salvation, unborn and unloved in an alien land,
Castaways forever wandering the limitless
Horizon, searching for the world we destroyed,
Consumed by fangs of shadow and bloodlust.

We are husks of our ancestors, withered shells
Wavering on scorched winds, senseless beings,
Numb to pain, programmed solely for survival,
Our receptors coded to self-destruct upon
Successful procreation, mechanical and artificial,
We trudge on, awaiting death's forbidden embrace.

# DEEP
# DOVER
# STOCK

# STRUCTURES

# Book Sale
## by Christine Kwon

Some people are unlikeable
before they die.
I am waiting for some
to go ahead.
Then I buy their book,
read their poems
and like them.
I guess I should say writers.
But I don't mean my friend in texas
or that one pretty branchlike girl in new york.
I don't mean you—
I mean the men and women
whose books I buy—
Who drank cocktails alone
at a café table,
Who sat by a pond crying
to the muse who beckoned
in the center,
Who wet the rich black fur
of their cat with hot tears,
Who burned their breakfast
looking at it,
Whose feet were cold
whisking back and forth the dark,
Who wanted to cry choosing a coat,
Who died penniless,
the absence of some drug
streaking down the veins
of one arm,
Who crowd my living room
threatening to bury me
with their excellence
with their clothed faces
and embossed eyes
and fat new yorker bellies,
Who greet me in the morning
sullenly as neglected housewives,

and say how lucky you are,
when you die
there will be a lovely book sale.

# The Capitol Dome
## by Mark Parsons

Ornate cloud of sharp angle-rife tube and clamp scaffold
Blurs dome
Like a JPEG-formatted digital photograph,
Heavy compression reducing the natural colour gradations and surface details
To illegible posterized script
Not even the Catalan architect Gaudi could read;
Vertical standards like ribs of a corset to bind up the sides of the Capitol Dome,
Reinforced horizontally
By right angle, cold drop-forged
Coupler-fast
Ledgers,
Tweak the circumference
And bevel its arc into increments,
Make multitudinous facets
The cross-braces zig-zag along
Like American shoelaces
Holding down leathery tongues
And inscribing their grooves as a pattern of
Obscure Norse
Runes
Carved in stone tablets.
From a distance the million-plus[-change] pounds
Of aluminum scaffolding
Bristles like chitinous setae, the outgrowths that nettle and fur
Exoskeletons arthropods wear,
An elaborate byzantine tortured mosaic of crosshatch so dense,
Fragile and delicate
Only incredible strength and stolidity
Could prevent
Hands that would hold from destroying
The tessellate meshwork of mortar and pestled till pulverized contours;
The fractures and splinters and slivers
Accelerate, propagate—
Shrink—

Geometrically,
Increase in number achieved
Through a decrease in size, granularity.
The veiled bell or pear shape
Like a jello mold, or an insect collagen aspic mold,
Composed of connected bays
(Three-dimensional reference areas
[Blocks of space]
To enable timely, effective
Tactical force direction, control, facilitate
Max-efficiency asset use
[Personnel and weaponry, ordnance and transport vehicles,
Combat casualty care and medicine]
Small rectangular zones,
Applied
To some quickly-drawn
Disposition matrix [or kill list]
That derived from life-style, behavior pattern
Analysis based
On a well-established and trusted formula, an age-old strategic tool
Harkening back to the past,
Grafted on spaces ungoverned—religiously, geopolitically, ideologically—
Used in order to pinpoint presence of
Enemy prey, and which prey
Carries around its own free-moving, mobile,
Or portable zone of hostility
[Unless the map
Gets confused
With the places rendered....]
A weapons-grade,
Algorithmically sound, military
Intelligence-backed,
On the fly
And immediate,
Moment-to-moment projection)
(Carved and stacked, piece-molding something
Complex and valuable)
Cantilevered to hug the decreasing perimeter:
Skirt to peristyle,
Boiler plate to the second story,
The belt course, cupola,

Tholos—all
Of it
Built on top
Of the inner dome—
You see, every dome's two
Cast iron domes
Painted
To match stone:
Each successive ring—
Architecture, ornament—breaking up,
Every decorative flourish, curlicue
Snapping off
Light and crumbly,
To show the honeycombed rust beneath
Paint
Pitted and pockmarked,
A thing
Buried a long time, hidden from sight.

# Storms Over Red Wing

## by Carolyn Adams

Mostly land and wind here.
Barns, silos, woodframe houses
float on a sea of plowed fields.
It's the last of winter,
not quite spring.

A storm's blown in tonight,
gusts slashing the house, crashing
the dead aspen onto the dairy shed roof.
Thunder rattles the loose sash
in the kitchen window.
Lightning rips tears in the black sky-plain above.
Out on the highway, semis like barges
navigate the channels
between undulating gray hills,
cloaked in rain.

Although it"s welcome in the fields
where crops wait,
like hope, to green and grow,
the downpour"s flooded the garden, muddied the road.

That roof will need repair tomorrow,
that tree, hauled away.

Cliff Dwellers - Carolyn Adams

# Oubliette

## by Justin Ratcliff

Body wrought chasm of derelict error
Pitch black prism of deranged terror
Memory lapsed transference of sooty bereavement
Satanic messenger sent to gift mind's diseased rent

Spiked baseboards; impale my misty soul
My flooded heart drowns; sheathed knoll
Salty tears cause the flood to score festering wounds
Wasted prayers castigate and reflect forgotten tombs

Deep divers cost of treasure troves entry
Lost are honorifics of the dubious gentry
I love the voided suffering of gnostic's nil perch
It all signifies and justifies my tortured lurch

Knee to chest, turmoil's closed casket of regress
Depressed to flesh, warband scalping innate tress
Held to press, a nuptial cloaked ingest
Detest, a vehement crucifixion's behest

Choke out all of pleasures, phallic, porridge
Shatter all mirroring, malignant, mooring
Breath in the tender lines of peaceful shoring
Accept the body as a member of triune glory

# DEEP OVERSTOCK

# In the Attic

## by Alan Brickman

Whenever Steve visited his brother Benny in Chicago, Benny's wife Cheryl, who never liked Steve, made him sleep in the attic. They had an extra bedroom, but that belonged to their daughter Barbara who was away at college and insisted that while she was gone, no one be let into her room, let alone sleep there. So, Steve was banished to the attic like some painful memory that Benny and Cheryl wanted to avoid by keeping it out of sight.

When Steve was first offered the mattress on the attic floor, he complained, "What am I, like Anne Frank, or something? In that case, make sure the Gestapo doesn't know I'm here!"

"What the hell is wrong with you?!" Cheryl roared. "That's really offensive." She turned to Benny, who was stifling a laugh, and said, "Tell your asshole brother to shape up, or he can go find a hotel room." She stormed off to their bedroom and slammed the door.

The next year, Steve visited in winter, during a cold snap, and it was off to the attic again. He was glad that it was nice and toasty up there, but when he saw a rat skitter across the floor in the corner, he went downstairs and slept on the couch. When Cheryl found him there in the morning, huddled under the blanket he dragged down from the attic, she went back into the bedroom and yelled at Benny. Steve couldn't make out what she was saying, but he could guess.

Now, several years and as many visits later, Steve was resigned to his banishment, and did his best not to antagonize or upset Cheryl, even though he knew he was always one misstep away from re-igniting her disdain, and that any real reconciliation was a long shot. They had a delicious dinner of Cheryl's chicken parmesan and finished two bottles of red wine that

Steve purchased earlier that day. They played Scrabble after dinner, and because Cheryl won a game when she put SQUAWKER on a triple word and scored over a hundred points, she was in such a good mood that she even hugged Steve before he headed upstairs.

He opened the attic door, ducked to avoid the low ceiling as he always did, and walked toward the mattress. He was startled to see the figure of a man sitting at the old desk that Benny and Cheryl kept up here. "Who are you? What are you doing here?" he blurted out. The man turned and Steve saw that it was his grandfather, who died many years ago right after he had just turned eighty-seven. Only this was not the octogenarian version of his grandfather, but a much younger man, no more than forty. He was wearing a red and green Hawaiian shirt and was smoking a cigar.

"Stevie," the man said. "It's me, Grandpa Joe. I live here now. I should be asking you what you're doing here. This is my room after all." He smiled.

"Grandpa?" Steve said, trying to take this in and make sense of it. "You live here? I was under the impression that you don't live anywhere, because you died in, what, like 1995? How long have you lived here? When did you move in?"

"I've lived up here ever since Benny and Cheryl moved to Chicago and bought the house. They picked this house because of the attic space, which was for me." His smile grew bigger. "And I must say that I'm surprised by your petulant attitude about these delightful accommodations."

"You're surprised?! I'm the one who should be saying that. This is totally... wait! Benny and Cheryl know you're here? And they made me sleep in the attic and didn't tell me. This is insane!"

"You'll have to ask them about that," said Grandpa. "Now go to sleep."

Steve slept fitfully and dreamed that a group of his relatives, all deceased, were chasing him like zombies, their rotting flesh dripping off them. The next morning, his grandfather was gone, and he hurried downstairs, anxious to talk to his brother and sister-in-law.

Benny said, "I know we drank a lot of wine last night, but Grandpa living in the attic? I think you're losing it."

Cheryl asked,

Are you okay, Steve?" with an uncharacteristic degree of genuine concern.

"I'm fine, I guess, but…"

Benny said, "You know that Grandpa died more than twenty years ago, right? After the funeral, Mom gave us a box full of his stuff, including photos of him and Grandma, and we keep *that* in the attic. The old photos are great! Their vacation in Puerto Rico, Grandpa with his coworkers at that furniture manufacturing company, graduation pictures from high school, college, and business school. There's a great photo of Grandpa holding you as a newborn, the first grandchild, and he was beaming! We should bring them down and go through them."

"Not right now," said Steve. "Maybe later."

That evening they went to the movies and saw "Kiss Kiss Bang Bang" with Robert Downey Jr. and Val Kilmer, and laughed all the way home in the car recounting the funniest scenes.

They had a nightcap sitting around the dining room table, and when Steve rose to go to the attic, Benny said, "Say hello to Grandpa." Steve scowled.

When he got to the top of the stairs, Steve hesitated before opening the attic door. He took a deep breath and went in. There was Grandpa, standing in front of the desk wearing a cap and gown and looking no more than twenty-five. Steve thought he appeared quite dashing with his movie-star good looks and a full head of hair. Steve had only known him as bald.

"Aren't you going to congratulate me?" said Grandpa.

"First college graduate in the family."

"Congratulations, I guess. By the way, you lied to me about Benny and Cheryl knowing you were up here." Grandpa shrugged and smiled. Steve said, "Can I ask you a question?"

"Sure," said Grandpa as he took off his mortarboard and sat in the chair by the desk.

"What the hell is going on? Are you alive? Are you dead? Are you a ghost?"

"Let me share my little secret with you. See that box over there?" He pointed to a plastic storage bin in the corner. "My whole life is in there. Pictures of it anyway. Whenever I feel like it, I select one and bring it to life. I stay up here in the attic because it's nice and cozy, and I can reminisce for a bit, even if it's just me, myself, and I. And Cheryl – dear old Cheryl, that delicate flower – she'd have a stroke if I showed up downstairs." He smiled. "I understand you and your sister-in-law don't get on that well."

"It's getting better," said Steve.

"Anyway, once I knew you'd be sleeping up here on a regular basis – because you finally accepted that it wasn't so terrible – I decided to show myself because, one, I thought you'd appreciate it, and, two, I would have somebody to talk to. I mean, here we are talking now and it's great! Now, if only I could get you to come here more than once a year."

"This is a lot to take in, don't you think?" said Steve, "But I do appreciate it. I was away in college when you …"

"Died," said Grandpa. "You can say it. I don't mind."

"When you died. It was during finals and I couldn't get away for the funeral. Which I felt terrible about."

"Don't worry about it," said Grandpa. "Some people came, some didn't. That's the way funerals are. And you know what? The guest of honor doesn't realize it and doesn't give a shit. 'Cause they're dead!" He threw his head back and laughed.

"So," said Steve. "Each night you come alive as a different one of the photos in the box and just sit here and think about the old days?"

"And now I can talk to you about 'em. You were always my favorite grandson anyway. Benny's a little dim, and he married that shrew Cheryl. And don't get me started on Barbara, the spoiled brat. Although I can thank her for one thing. Because her bedroom has been declared the sanctum sanctorum, you have to sleep up here. With me!"

Steve knew none of this made any sense, but he was pleased to be told he was the favorite, and charmed by his grandfather's attitude. He stood, walked toward the desk, and offered to shake hands. When Grandpa put out his hand, Steve's passed through it as if it were smoke. Grandpa laughed. "I'm only spectral, Steve. An apparition. Sorry about that."

Steve stepped back, and sat on a stack of boxes against the wall and rubbed his eyes. "Okay then, tell me some stories. Tell me about college, now that you've graduated and all."

"Lots of unchaperoned co-eds, Stevie. That was the best part. The *very* best part."

And the two of them talked until well into the next morning.

# The Identity Card
## by Maumil Mehraj

It was perhaps one of the only times when your own heartbeat was not reassuring. Under the sky so blue it would pierce your eyes, bluer than the color of his very eyes, he felt life slowly leave his limbs. If Ali were any younger, younger by just a day, he would have let his fear seep from out of his body, and onto his shorts – a shameful act of being what they called human. But he couldn't do that. Only yesterday, had Ali become a man of 11 years. He knew it so well because his mother had taken him to the shrine of Makhdoom Saeb and pronounced him a man henceforth. He had returned home older, more responsible, suddenly. The heart that was in him was impudent, beating – fast – despite his many admonitions; it would give him away.

It was not a day where anyone, let alone the beloved Ali, should have fallen on the ground. Ali, the pride and joy of his parents, who would get an education and get them out of poverty. He had the eyes that demanded respect, even though they were a child's eyes. This morning, he had woken up particularly early because they had announced on TV that it was going to be a hot day and he wanted to take a bath before going to school. He was that child – wanting to better himself for others' happiness, however childlike that thought might have been. Others should feel happy when they look at me, he thought. Sacrificing an hour of sleep, he awoke, and turned on the geyser to heat the water up. In Kashmir, it was silly to think of taking a cold bath, even in summer months.

Before he dressed, Ali powdered himself up, and one could still see the white dust above the collar of his shirt. Perhaps he had done that on purpose, to let people know that he was clean and powdered. He wouldn't know what the day would bring for him, despite all his carefulness. One last look in the mirror, he told himself. He was 11, Ali, and quite short for his age, but he did not mind that so much – it meant he got to stand in front of the assembly line at school. His white button-down shirt, part of his school uniform, was ironed to perfection, unlike some of his peers', and his shorts just touched his knees. He was a good kid, he genuinely believed so. And he had to be; he did not know from where he got this idea, but he wanted to be the one who would bring his family out of poverty – not his brother, nor his sister. Him.

He walked by the same set of houses he always did, read the same posters on the electricity poles he always did – that freedom was near. He couldn't see it yet. But something was off about that day. Anxious, he began reviewing in his head the material for the English test his teacher was sure to give today. But, for some reason, his anxiety never went away. This was unlike Ali. He was usually just the right amount of confident, and for good reason, too. Ali would always study for his tests, he would remember to go to the kandur at 5 pm each day to bring bread for the evening tea. He never forgot to turn off the geyser after his bath, and never left his window open after the sun set for mosquitoes and spirits alike to enter.

His school was not too far away from home, so he walked. He saw Saleem on the way. Saleem was a youth who was incurably sick in his mind, or so the elders told him. He would ask everyone who would listen to buy him a movie ticket. He did not – could not – understand the cinema halls had long been closed.

"Yes, Saleem, after I come back from school, I will get you a ticket."

Ali said a quick goodbye because he was always scared of offending Saleem or frightening him.

"I will wait for my ticket," he shouted as Ali sped past.

Ali's mother was beautiful, one of the most beautiful women he had ever seen. As he was walking, his mind went to her struggles. Rifat had always had a smiling face – people said that was the reason why she had developed her smile lines so early on in life. Her small hands had hardened from washing in the cold water, and then his mind wandered to how she would only buy cheap fabric from the road-side stalls for her dresses. There was a feeling of comfort she carried which Ali could not quite explain, maybe she had dreams as well – what kind of dreams, it was a secret to all but herself. Her beautiful face would always smile; his dutiful heart would always beat.

At the turn, there was some sort of a water body. Common knowledge has it that this used to be a part of the Dal Lake, and an echo of the old glory remained, but to Ali, this was just the water in front of his school, unceremonious, not given a grand title of a forgotten inheritance. But at this turn, on this day, everything went wrong. His school was a few footsteps away, he could see his classroom windows on the second floor from where he was standing. But the road was barricaded, and several men in uniform, looking grossly out of place, and really, stupid in their self-importance, walked about. He did not care for this, and decided to take the much longer route to his classroom. Vexation, at her best.

One of the uniformed men, a tall thing of twenty-five or so, was standing in the self-imposed solitude of his bunker. Ali saw him lodge a mighty finger into his nostril and go at it with a warrior's determination. It was a surprise that a finger that fat could fit into his nose. The nostril started to swell immediately on impact, and made way, accommodating the mammoth digit. Indeed, the man in uniform was so fixated on the task that it was only a few seconds later that he saw Ali looking. Shamed by his own blurring of the public and the private, he thought it appropriate to take it out on the child. Before he knew it, Ali was thrown onto the ground by a slap that would go on to hurt his cheek for days.

"Hasta hai?" the man in uniform asked, "will you laugh at me?"

Ali was, at this point, more annoyed than scared. He had made it a point to leave home early so he would reach school before time. But now, not only was he going to be late, but his uniform – his angelic white – had become almost as dusty and devilish as his aggressor's. He tried in vain to explain that he wasn't laughing, it was like talking to a wall, a boundary, a barbed wire, an inanimate division. A kick to the stomach. He could see nothing but the man's boots – big, perhaps too big for the wearer? Black, unnatural, they were a monstrosity, worn not to protect, but to hurt. He wondered if they hurt him, too. All these thoughts vanished and as his senses returned, he was able to feel the pain. His cheek was burning, and shame accompanied the sting. He was a good kid, he never received so much as a scolding, and now, here he was, on the ground, bloody and defeated. The man was saying something, but through the prison of his helmet, words came slow and thoughtless.

"ID dikha," he demanded from the child, "show me your ID."

Ali's hand went involuntarily to his breast pocket, where he, where every man, every boy, kept the proof of his being. He was. He existed. He could prove it. But he only heard a sorry beating of his heart instead – fast, eager to please – this was a boy's heart.

In a moment of inexplicable fear, he realized that the piece of paper that made him who he was, was not there. He had forgotten it at home. It came back to him in torrents – he had taken his ID out the previous night – he washed his shirts every two days, but ironed them every night. Before ironing, he had removed his ID card, and kept it safely on an inverted glass in the kitchen.

"ID," he yelled. It would be long before he knew that this word would echo in his ears for the years to come – perhaps all his life. Ali did not have his ID, he was not there, not him; a mass of bone and skin took his place. That day, Ali missed his English test. He did not buy bread at 5 pm, and there was nobody to close the window at sundown. It was the first of many.

# DEEP OVER STOCK

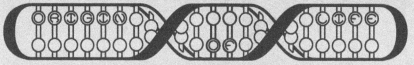

# The Eves
## by Olive Wexler

if you ever leave me
I'm coming with you
pass me the fruit
we can shed our old skin

I won't mind
the bitter bite
the second slice

we wasted years
not knowing
but I've always been curved
at your side

you build the fire
I'll suck the marrow from the bones
We'll be possessed with ourselves
no exorcism needed

don't water the garden
just take a bucket to catch the rain
and maybe an apple for the road

# origin story
## by BEE LB

*after Karin Gottshall*

lake superior whispered me into existence, from dream
to bodily dream. my body was never meant to be so far
from the water. but so it goes.

summer of 1997, a year early and a little extra change.
my mother was round with life, my father ripe
with the stench of possibility. a month or two out
from crumbling beneath themselves.

the rusted signs pointing home. did success live already
in the confines of meth trailers? i could ask, but what would be
the point. i like to think this was before the world went bad
though the world went bad long before any living memory.

the sorrow of it all. the wasted potential. i imagine my mother's eyes
glazing past the water stretching toward the skyline, stuck instead
to the hot sand beneath her feet. she never learned to swim
and we are all weak swimmers as a result. for her it was never

a matter of fear. somehow, the water never called to her. the water
doesn't speak to me, but i hear it all the same. the changing of life
from possibility to responsibility happened some feet away from
lake superior. it is a slow change. one i denied for as long as i could.

i kept a drowning gown in the back of my closet. it did not go untouched,
but it did go unused. not the first, but one of many unforgivable mistakes.

that summer spent drinking and smoking and gambling and hiding.
that summer spent digging my blunt nails against rock formation.
that summer spent rushing through the forest to my favorite secret.

we've jumped so far ahead. what of the becoming?

there's only so many ways one can say,
for my body to be given one had to be taken.
a misunderstanding of the way the world works
and yet, one i must have been born with.

my mother, round with life. my father, alone in a cell.
the distance that shaped me. often a gift, but not then.

there was no sorrow to be found in that moment, so
it all crawled into me, the smallest, most needful container.

origin is an entry. what becomes of the exit? it must be named a
wound.

# Conversations in a Graveyard

by Daniel J. Nickolas

Elephants and eyelash mites, streams of life,
Of heritage both mighty and minute,
Existence spies through milky eyes in strife,
Cascades in raging sound—genetic root;
The song, the strife, the milky streams all end
And yet that end comes as a mystery
—The wintry absence of breath—
You are the dark, against which we defend
Without victory through our blind alchemy;
We'll rest in the garden you keep, nigh Death.

We practiced the constructs of tradition:
Etched granite stone that lets us remember
And hides the decay of Your condition—
Pyres that lift the soul on pulsing embers,
Sweet platitudes that make our loss seem fair;
The urn, the casket, veil of shoveled earth
There to see, but not to look.
Yet for our work, tradition leaves us bare:
Nothing more than a blind and fragile mirth—
The hiding of a flower in a book.

Yet it's the still rocks who feed the lichen—
The old trees, when scorched, who enrich the soil
Which grows the grass of the fields we lie in,
Crafts the loam that lets the fern's frond uncoil.
Are our bodies the rocks, the wood aflame?
A nourishment, a balm, a new rhythm?
Yes, You give us a new name;
From one comes many—light through a prism—
You, Death—the one who will not be sated—
Are the dust from which we are created.

# born
## by Clarissa Grunwald

in the beginning, there was a river and
an old man in a rowboat fishing
the hazel water for coins and feathers and things
and there was you,

in the silt, all twisted up in soda rings
with the hook burrowed deep in the red flesh of your foot.

so he dragged you out; you sprawled on the stones
where the first green things had begun to grow
and the old man put down his fishing pole
and dragged his rotting boat
underground

# Sand Mandala With Ancestral Names
by Kate Falvey

*for Anna Laura Grace Elena*

The crushed rubies and sweet woodruff are Angelina,
who died of her ninth bambino, making a bed of her
memory for her two-year-old Laura who would see
her mother's ghost ever after on the landing, backlit
by gaslight and need.

The lapis lazuli and bluebells are Annie, Angelina's
seventh-born who died of a kitchen-table appendectomy,
making a veil of her memory for Laura, her sister, to wear
in perpetual mourning and for her little niece Elena to
feel ethereal whispers of tender angelic regard.

The citrine and thyme are Laura, Angelina's last child,
Annie's sister, mother of Elaine, who lived in the glare of the
the sun with her shades for one hundred years, making a fist
and a wink of her memory for her children to learn to
pronounce
themselves with effervescent fortitude and steely, vigorous joy.

The opal and lavender are Elaine, Angelina's granddaughter,
Laura's daughter, Annie's niece, who offers her ninety-five years
as a testament to intelligent kindness and self-determination,
making a cradlesong of her memory to keep her children safe
in the lilt of her boundless and deathless belief.

The turquoise and sage are Ellen, Angelina's great-
granddaughter, Laura's granddaughter, Elaine's daughter,
Anna Laura's mother, who is here still, her heart scarred and
toughened with surgical scars and devotion, making a moon
of her memory to light her daughter's way home.

# Cremation
## by John Delaney

We watched the pine box enter,
the door close,
and then the jets of the burners roared.
'Through hell he goes,'

I thought. And how we stood
together silently,
hearing the flames consume
so violently

the stoic man that was our dad.
It wouldn't take long
to reduce his 90 years to ashes,
everything he held right or wrong.

I like to think we felt a modicum of warmth disperse
across the cold, unloving universe.

# DEEP OVER STOCK

# ANIMALS

# Self-Portrait as Angler Fish
## by Cecily Cecil

You say maybe we can't be friends because
you think I can't express anger.
You have a degree in psychology.
Anger is important to you.

But Anger is a tsunami—
a greedy, gluttonous predator—
an indifferent drowner of you and
me.
Anger is an insatiable carnivore,
but since you're angling for anger, let
me imagine
what it would be like to be carnivorous for a day.
When your words bite, to plunge through the depths
on my bloated belly, to unhinge my gaping maw, to portend
perfect pearlescent protuberances,
only for you to realize that I drew your bite
with the cruel intent to absorb everything you are.
Lured by dangling dorsal brilliance—
my pulsing luminescence nothing more than foul fleshy growth,
cultured bacteria in an esca.
What if that were my angle?
But if you become my symbiote,
isn't empathy inevitable?
So then can't we just skip over all the anger and be friends?

# The Ape
## by Eric Thralby

*Inspired by "The Cape."*
   In the wind of the beach, I climbed into the gorilla.
   Its skin hung down like an immense human cape.
         --Ben Crowley


   My father always knocked on my door. 'Perchance, the ape is in?'

   He opened my door and helped me into the costume. He beat a drum and said, Ladies and Gentlemen... The Ape.

   I tumbled, I dragged my knuckles, I oogabooga'd.

   I left school and learned to operate the roller coaster. We too, at our county fair, had an ape. He stalked the children and stole their bananas. He wore a tie and could stand on a ball.

   Once, the ape attacked me. He pinned me to the ground under the scrambler. He spit a long stream of candy through his mask and into my mouth. 'Welcome to Stan Land,' he said. His name was Stanley, the Ape.

   'I've seen the ape,' I told my father over the phone.

   'Again?' he said.

   'Yes,' I said.

   He said, 'God, gotta love the ape. What's he say? Ooga-booga?'

   'Yes,' I said.

   My father's voice became small. 'Your own ape's here, you know. Just getting dusty.'

# The Return of the Ape
## by Eric Thralby

When the circus burned down, I found work selling peanuts.

Here on the boardwalk people purchased day-old sardines in order to feed the pelican, sticking their arms up to their shoulders into its throat. Patient old bird.

Unfortunately, there was a balloon man.

'What do you say I fold you a big banana?' he said.

'No,' I said.

The balloon man had a secret. 'I have a little son.'

'I will not patronize an ape,' I said.

'Here he is,' he said.

His little son tumbled and hooted like a monkey. He could balance on a ball.

He was everything an ape should be. But with no costume, he was just an ordinary boy.

I called my father on a phone by the pier. There was a long pause at first. I could say nothing and my father only muttered confusedly into the phone. Finally, I gave him the truth.

'Oogabooga,' I said.


When my father arrived in a cloud of dust and his sky-blue van, I introduced the balloon man to my father and the balloon man introduced my father to his little son.

My father hunched and crinkled a small paper bag. 'I've got something here for you, my boy,' said my father to the boy.

My father removed the ape from the paper sack. It was like a real animal. Its feet dangled as they slipped past the edge of the sack. 'Do you think maybe he can try it on?'

The balloon man took the ape suit from my father and pressed his thumbs into it as if assessing its quality. 'Boy,' was all he said.

The boy climbed into the ape, then stood on the ball.

We stood around the small ape on the ball, going around and around, rocking the planks of the boardwalk. The boy rolled off the ball and into a somersault. He hooted and hollered, heavily tiptoeing and tickling his own underarms.

The two fathers enjoyed it so much. They slapped at their thighs and thumbed away tears. A crowd gradually drifted in like the tide, the pier creaking under its weight.

In all the excitement, I finally escaped.

# Traces
## by Kate Falvey

A gorilla
zooed in a kindly habitat
not quite like
its mountained own
recently cradled a fallen
human infant, unused to heights
and jarred from its slip
away from mother's arms.
The gorilla, a mother herself,
understood yowling when she heard it.
She set the child before the keeper's gate,
assuming kind
should go
immaculate to kind,
knowing the bandied creature
would be
stumbled upon and pet
when the evening bananas
were tumbled in.

Rejoicing all round,
scratches dressed
and diapers changed,
and new takes
on animal altruism
extended from
this interface.

It might have been
a fluke, a particularly gentle
and bright gorilla, or, conversely,
one too instinctively pea-brained
to figure out a scheme
for stealing and storing
this morsel-from-the-skies,
or, was she an impish sort,
nursing a secret lauding over

her condescending captors --
vengeance tempting but
not sporting -- or worth
the aggravation,
or, maternally pragmatic, she
could surely have been one
who'd simply had enough
monkeys on her back
to trouble with another.
She may only
have wanted to
get rid of all the
racket.

Experimental infants
might be sacrificed
to science, flung one
by squalling one
to a statistically viable
assortment of gorillas, varied
in species, gender, rank, and age,
place, origin, rearing,
and type, if any,
of human influence and contact,
to gather more conclusive
comparative data.
Just so we'd know
for sure
why this quirk happened.

But this is all
indulgent
by-the-way. I'd rather
wax speculative
about the
rescued child.

How will he
mature
with this story
as his climate?
Always a kind of
temperature-controlled

landscape of fright and
hairy arms, some ur-memory
of eyes near golden
in recognition and
lament.

Folk sucked down
fairy holes
who live to tell
the tale
never can quite
tell it. They
see things
they know they
remember
though it is
impossible
that they do.

# Guest
## by Carolyn Adams

The clock in the hall marks
each drowsing hour,
and the housecat keeps watch.
Tucked under a warm blanket
and pastel sheets, I sleep and dream.
In the morning, there's coffee
and quiet conversation,
here with my family that isn't blood
but family the same.
We'll sit on the porch in the sun
and watch for the rabbit that lives in the yard
as it travels its wild route
through the garden, under the steps
where the tulips will bloom,
and up on the deck, to stand
and watch us, twitching its velvet ears.
Looking me over,
learning who I am, adding me to the roster
of who is welcome here.

# Part of Darkness
## by AJD

Jack and I followed the creek for half an hour. Once in a while we peered past the clumps of bushes and trees along the embankment, frustrated that we could still catch glimpses of picnic tables or awnings or trailers, the glint of trucks or cars or bikes. Soon, we hoped, the stream would lead us out of the hillbilly resort, past the smell of barbecues, the sound of transistor radios and portable TVs, to our goal, the woods.

Jack was my best friend. He had come with my family to our small, recently acquired "camping" trailer outside the small town of Brookville, Indiana for a three-day vacation. The entire summer was a vacation for Jack and me. We were twelve, and though Jack did sports and I had band camp, these things did not tie us down, at least not this early in the summer.

After wading knee-deep through murky water topped with an industrial waste sheen, we were finally able to slip under a dilapidated wire fence and exit the trailer park. Brown tadpoles wiggled lethargically over my tennis shoes as I sucked my feet up from the sludge and started an ascent into scrub forest.

The stream narrowed to a mere foot and a half across and became increasingly difficult to follow due to a heavy undergrowth of roots, branches, and vines. Eventually, a festoon of sticker bushes separated Jack and me. I lost sight of the water and, while turning and disoriented, almost walked into a low branch. I froze as a vine on top of the branch seemed to move. My eyes jerked over and focused on a tiny reptilian head, about three inches from my shoulder.

I backed into the stickers and called to Jack.

We studied the snake and discussed it like the seasoned outdoorsmen we pretended to be. We knew nothing about snakes and other such beasts, of course, except what we had seen on Mutual of Omaha's Wild Kingdom. Still, we bluffed our way through a long discussion, including some unlikely previous experiences.

After the snake spiraled off and I pulled free of the bush, our conversation progressed faster than our pursuit of the dwindling trickle. We moved from poisonous snakes to arm-wrenching snapping turtles to alligators and crocodiles and walked about 20 feet.

Abruptly, we came upon a small, mossy pond. It was only six feet across at its widest. I stood on the edge, estimating the water's depth, beginning to sweat in the late morning humidity, when the stillness erupted in a sharp pop. I gasped and jumped back. The sound echoed away, along with little waves from the center of the pond. Jack laughed.

For the next several minutes, we lit firecrackers and tossed them towards the pond, trying to make them explode as close as possible to the surface, leaving behind shreds of paper and puffs of bluish smoke. Enjoying our sport, we also surveyed our small enclosure of woods and pond.

Jack saw it first, even though it was closer to me.

Ahead of me an on my right—atop a mound of mossy mud about five feet away, staring towards the nearby water's edge about—sat the frog.

"Hey, watch this." Jack stalked past me and stole in behind his prey.

"No way, man. You'll never get it."

Undaunted, Jack crept in behind the frog. He slid his hand forward, very slowly. He got closer and closer. I was certain the frog would jump away, but it didn't. Jack lodged a firecracker in the mud directly beneath the frog's dark green backside. Only the fuse and a little of the firecracker's red paper remained visible.

He chuckled smugly. His display of steady-handed skill had impressed me as well.

"Hey, let me light it."

"No way! Find your own frog!"

Jack fumbled for the matches, but I knew who had them.

"Heh, heh, heh, heuhmm!" I let out a slow snicker, waiting for recognition. "That's right. Moi. I'll light this one."

I had the matches, but Jack the position. There followed a short, bitter argument.

Persistence, along with an embarrassing willingness to grovel, triumphed.

Now it was my turn to sneak up on this strange little amphibian. The marshy ground sucked at feet already encased in several layers of earth. I lay down my knee, elbow. I sank into the mire and leaned forward. At last in position, I struck a match against the book I held in my left hand.

It went out.

The next five also refused to remain lit long enough to do the job. I made a neat pile of their useless bodies. It wasn't windy, the matches just kept going out before I could get them to the fuse. Jack muttered curses behind my back as I realized I didn't have many matches left.

I guided my hand steadily with the next one, cradling the little blue and yellow fire against the non-existent gale with a cupped hand. I had it just beneath the gray paper coil of the fuse when the flame crawled back towards the head of the match and retreated into dead ember. Disgusted, I tossed the match into the pond.

I turned my head sharply back down.

Jesus! The frog still hadn't moved. Was this thing alive or what? It sat there oblivious to our attempts to blast it into orbit. I monitored it closely until I made sure that its dark back and pale stomach moved in a way that indicated it was taking tiny little breaths. I tore off the second to the last match. Jack kicked my foot to tell me I'd better make it work.

I struck the match and set it quickly to the fuse. It lit.

Now, now the frog would jump for sure! A hot, unnaturally forged instrument of death burned just below, a half-inch beneath. The frog had to feel the heat and know something was wrong, that its life was somehow being threatened.

It would have to notice that!

"Jump!" I screamed.

It sat there perfectly calm, paying us no mind whatsoever. With a moment of fuse remaining, I leaned backwards and shut my eyes.

Pop. Silence. With the sharp ring dying in my ears, I opened my eyes onto a small crater, empty except for a bit of shredded red and white paper. The fertile looking mud slowly started to fill up the empty space. Speechless, I looked back at Jack who came and crouched next to me.

"Where'd it go?" I asked.

"You didn't see it? You were sitting right there!"

Jack was incredulous. Neither of us had seen it. There were no ripples on the pond, no dripping green bits in the branches just above our heads and definitely nothing in the subtle indentation that had once been the explosion crater—that had once been the frog.

"I thought something flew up, maybe, over there" Jack said, standing. "If that was him, he could be anywhere. To the moon, even, cause nothing came down, at least from what I saw."

After a pause when we began to take in the shock of the act, we initiated the grim search. A few minutes of mercifully unsuccessful reconnaissance later and I felt content to sit on a log at the edge of the tree line. It was there I saw it. It lay on top of a mushy patch of what looked like old cow paddy, or drying mud, some feet to the side of the log.

"He's over here." I said, feigning nonchalance.

Jack strode over quickly and I pointed over.

"Eeyuk."

"Yeah, he's not even dead yet. Look."

We peered at the yellow, phlegm-like guts, flowering out of the mid-section up to the large head. The mouth was open and would gape larger every few seconds to let out a pitiful, "Croak."

I wished he would croak for real.

"Just think," Jack said, "we're getting a head start on next year's biology."

"C'mon, we gotta finish him off."

"O.K., we got one more match left, right? You put a firecracker in his mouth and I'll . . ."

"No way! Let's just get a rock and drop it on him."

"Whatever."

We looked, but the best we could come up with were four stones that were smaller than our fists. We each took two and stood on opposite sides.

"Well, you first. Rocks were your idea."

I aimed and threw one of my rocks; it missed by at least a foot. Jack, splattered with muck, prepared a return volley. He also missed the target, but succeeded in splattering me. Our last two rocks were rapidly dispatched, leaving us covered with sticky earth or manure, but, thankfully, no frog remains.

Unfortunately, my last throw did manage to pin a leg deep into the mud, bringing up the head which pointed skyward at an angle. The tongue was now visible, hanging from the corner of the pale, fragile looking mouth and jaw.

The beast still croaked pitifully, but not with the finality I desired.

Jack held out a firecracker as if it were the Final Solution. I ignored him and looked around. The log was better, I thought.

We pulled and tugged and lifted, struggling like titans to position the ominous, decaying black cylinder above the green and yellow slime thing. We let go, hoped gravity would do the rest. Somehow, it was off by a few inches. It landed and rolled until our frog was no longer in sight, leaving a short trail of bugs and bark.

I kneeled behind the log's short trail and looked across the lake, seeking some sort of answer from the woods, wood nymphs, or Indian spirits. I turned my head back down and rolled the decayed bole aside to check on the remains. A few strands of snot-like guts stuck to the wood and some stayed on the ground. Beneath it all was our nemesis—the indestructible, suffering frog. He lay flush now, but his neck and head were still visible. He seemed to be gulping in preparation for another croak.

Damn! I had had too much. I rolled the log back over and jumped up and down on it with a nearly unhinged frenzy.

Jack was already walking and the trees consumed him before I felt finished and ready to follow.

On the way back, I detoured around the spot where I thought the snake would be. Somehow, I was certain he would know of the act I had just participated in, and that Karma might play some foul surprise on me. I had previously felt the same way after killing some ant or fly. I knew that the victim's companions were subsequently buzzing or crawling about me on a purposeful harassment campaign, founded on vengeance. Now, the frog—natural enemy of the insect—also had reason to hate me. Perhaps other amphibians and reptiles knew about us, the frog slayers. I walked a little faster, and got scratched a little more.

GOD! Even the plants were against me!

We left the stream at the first glimpse of corrugated metal. We cut through a corn field and scrambled over the fence early, bypassing the toxic sludge and its doomed inhabitants. In a construction area for new trailer lots, an ATV and two dirt bikes cut through along a rutted, dirt and gravel lane. We followed the dust back into our semi-populated RV resort, back to the Country Caravan Trailer we called home sometimes. My dad was grilling some hamburgers and the transistor radio crackled out a Reds game—the local heroes were winning. We were back.

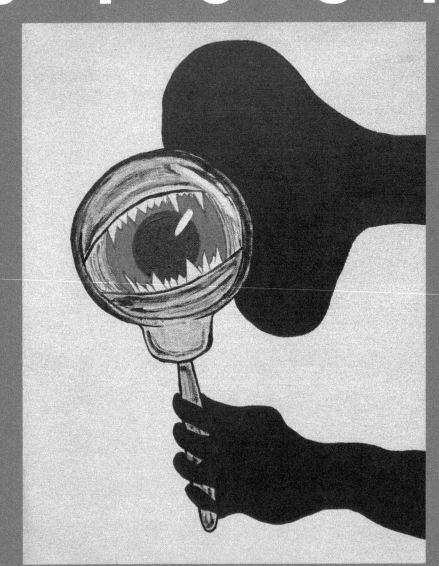

# The Loaf
## by Elizabeth Templeman

It sat precisely balanced atop a high concrete curb along the roadside, this perfect loaf of sliced white bread. How astonishing is that? Such an improbable, yet ordinary, place for such a commonplace thing as a loaf of bread.

But this was no ordinary, run-of-the-mill white bread. It was that Italian brand with the green and red logo. Someone had paid top dollar for this. I started to imagine that person: a mother with a houseful of young kids; or a twenty-four-year-old guy living on his own, hungry for a cheese sandwich, or two.

How on earth did the bread get *here*, resting on a sun-warmed curb dividing the busy bike and pedestrian lane that began, just at this point, to follow the North Thompson River? That's what I wondered, as I pedaled past. The homes, after all, are all along the other side of the road. On this side runs the trail, unspooling along the riverside. All that could be seen were a lone runner loping past a young couple pushing a stroller, and riding out ahead of them, my husband. It was not quite noon, and cool, on this fine Saturday morning.

I couldn't get the loaf out of my mind. It made no sense. Had a dog dragged it across the road, the plastic would have been punctured. And no dog would leave it perched on the concrete, perfectly aligned with the curb. Even an impeccably well-mannered dog would have nosed the thing, pulled or poked at the plastic with a paw. The loaf had appeared for all the world to have been *placed* there.

My mind toyed with the image, not unlike that dog would have toyed with the object. Who had placed it there? Why? And what of the person I now imagined to have made a Saturday morning trip to the grocery store to pick it up?

Someone clearly had wanted this loaf of bread; someone

would be missing it. At this exact moment, possibly. The idea of that loss tugged at me. I wanted to see if my husband had noticed, and what he'd thought. While I am known for *not* noticing—for oblivion to my environment, especially when in motion—he notices everything. Me? I tend to retreat to the comfort of my innermost thoughts, and to bicycle, run, hike, or ski in utter seclusion. Which might make me less than the ideal companion.

But on this morning I longed to share, and I tucked this small sad mystery in a corner of my mind. We were ten minutes into our one hour ride (which will be 59 minutes and 53 seconds this particular Saturday in September, for any who might obsess about such details). It's a sweet ride, too, winding out and back along the river trail, and then beneath a bridge, through a few quiet city blocks, to loop around a sports park, and return to the parking lot where our vehicle awaits.

Some twenty minutes later, I'm still trailing my husband, who's rounded back out to where bike lane meets road. I'm pushing to catch up, with about twenty meters of trail between us. The effort required to close the gap between us and also to pay some attention again to things like traffic and direction pulls me back from the recesses of my mind. On the river side of the trail, to my left, a woman rides past me. She's riding, or driving, what looks like a cross between a cart and a wheelchair. She sits back, low to the ground, her brown hair streaming out behind her. She holds a leash, and a gangly chocolate lab runs along beside her, between us. I take this in, and become vaguely aware that she's looking directly at me.

This can happen when I run or walk, too. I always feel solitary in the world; alongside others, but happily alone. It always takes me by surprise—is not unlike a tiny shock—to realize someone is connecting: maybe with a simple wave, or a comment about my t-shirt, or the weather. I don't know why I forget to expect this social connectedness that our species supposedly thrives on. But not even six decades of tipping inward has accustomed me to the jolt of reconnecting, socially. It's as though I'm one with the universe; but not quite so, with humanity.

This woman, with a broad smiling face, eyes seeking mine, is speaking. To me. Only as we pass one another do I hear her words: "I found my bread," she says. And again, for whatever reason, she chooses to say (to me!) "I *found* my bread."

The mystery is solved! I am awash with joy to know that the person who'd been missing her newly purchased loaf of bread has found it. Neither of us will know how the bread made its way up onto the curb. But we have shared, however incongruously, this surge of contentment.

It's a rare and beautiful thing, when the universe delivers a story, perfectly packaged. And *this* story has seemed for all the world to drop right out of the sky. A blessing, fully formed—not unlike a loaf of bread.

# This Screaming Mad//man
## by BEE LB

*a found poem, after Giannina Braschi*

Madmen fear no moon, fear no fire.
Burns of flesh are poetry. Madmen's wounds are poetry.
Salt is for fish, salt is for
death, the poem is not among the dead. Remember, but don't write it.
sleepwalker
among cats, thief among dogs, man among women, woman among men
blasphemous toward religion, fed up with poverty.
Don't let her find you, hide. Disregard her, ignore her, forsake her. no
touch her wounds, she'll scorn you. Backaway. Scorn the poem. Develop
without her. Give him the necessary distance.
insult her for not having written with power. Deride him from his
dreams from her,
Take the poem from his belly from her.
Sleep beside him, but don't take your eyes off her. Listen to what he tells
you in
dreams.
Descend with her into hell, climb its streets, burn within her history.
there
are no names, no history.
I can't do anything but bash her against a rock. I can't do anything but
hug her. I can't do anything but insult her dreams of her, and he can't do
anything but open the poem for me, just a crack, half-said, in silence,
to keep distant, to keep
silent, to appear barefoot. And she couldn't do anything
and time
couldn't do anything but eternalize
And poetry is nowhere
disappears through the trapdoor, escapes with the fire that
burns her and dissolves in water.

# DEEP
# OVER
# STOCK

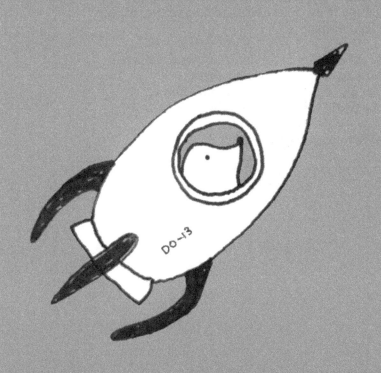

# FUTURE

# I Left Your Keys on the Kitchen Table

by Carella Keil

Time is a rabbit that won't stop jumping
A forest of broken lamps.
I caught you in the corner of my eye
Pulled you in like a sunken star ship.
*
It's summertime in another dimension.
I left my front door unlocked and all the furniture
walked away.

The cat is napping on the windowsill. Galaxies
float past her and she swats them
away like dust motes. You should know
Love is still the hardest word to pronounce.

I have to wear armor while I dream.

# my robot
## by Mark DeCarteret

got caught
on a not so
hidden camera
his eyes these
two dots &
his surface
so white it
fought off any light
his sound bit-
ten off as he
tried telling them
how he'd gotten
the notebook
so he could
jot down all
he thought were
his own thoughts
but were now
virtually
nothing worth
noting lots of
zeros & ones
our hero now
re-dotting his eyes
his surface so
white he could be
spotted from
atop the clouds
what had pass
worded off
for an identity--
all he'd been taught
about being an "I"
bought into ever-
y thing they
were selling

# Ricky's Magic Powers
## by Alan Brickman

Ricky smiled after doing it successfully ten times in a row. He could move the card from one hand to the other so that it couldn't be seen, and he didn't need any misdirection to do it. He had been practicing a card trick that involved this new sleight-of-hand for the better part of a week, and he finally felt ready for an audience. He looked in the mirror. He was dressed for performance – crisp white shirt, bow tie, his best shoes polished to a shine. He checked the pockets of his jacket to make sure he had everything he needed. He walked confidently downstairs and called his parents into the living room.

"Pick a card," he said to his father.

"Let your mother do it. She's the one who likes magic tricks. I always figure them out, so I don't really enjoy it." Ricky's father hadn't changed out of his work clothes, but his tie was loosened and the top button of his shirt was undone. Ricky thought his father seemed different these past few weeks, grumpier. Something had happened at work. Ricky heard his parents arguing about it a few nights ago, but he didn't know what it was. His father walked to the other side of the room and dropped himself into his favorite chair.

"George, don't be such a drip," Ricky's mother said. George waved her off. She turned to her son. "I'll do it, honey. Your father seems to have decided that being cynical and above-it-all is the very essence of wisdom." His father scowled and picked up the newspaper from the coffee table.

"Thanks, Mom." Ricky fanned the deck in one hand and held it out. "Pick a card."

His mother leaned in and looked up at Ricky with a big smile before she drew a card. Ricky thought his mother looked dowdy in her house dress and the apron she still had on since dinner. It made her seem an easy mark, trusting and gullible.

"Show it to Dad." She held up the card and Ricky's father rolled his eyes in a melodramatic show of indifference, even as he nodded.

"Alright," said Ricky. He waved his hand and looked around the room as if speaking to a much larger audience. "Has everyone seen the card? Dad?"

"Yes!" his father snapped, making clear how disinterested and put upon he was.

"Okay," said Ricky. "Mom, now take this marker and write your name on the card." She took the pen and signed her name with a theatrical flourish. Ricky said, "Fold the card twice and hold it tightly in your hand." She followed his instructions. He drew a wand from his jacket and waved it over her closed fist. Her hand seemed very small, like a child's, something he'd never noticed before.

"I've seen this one and I know how it's done," Ricky's father said. He stood as if to leave.

Ricky felt the anger rising in his throat. "Dad! Why are you being like this?! You ruin everything!" Without thinking, he threw the deck of cards right at his father's face. His mother gasped. The cards flew everywhere. As the last one fluttered to the ground, Ricky's father coughed as if something were caught in his throat. He reached into his mouth and pulled out a folded playing card.

"What the hell is this?" He unfolded the card and held it up. His wife's name was written in black marker.

"Mom, open your hand," Ricky said. She did. It was empty.

The three of them stood in stunned silence. Ricky's mother mouthed the word, "Wow," and almost began clapping, but looked at her husband and thought better of it. Ricky's father was fuming, but he also looked puzzled as he tried to figure out what just happened. Ricky had no idea how the card ended up in his father's mouth, but he was glad it did. "So, Dad, if you're so smart, tell me how it was done."

"Go to your room, young man. I'll deal with you later." He looked at his wife, whose face was now etched with alarm. "Doris, clean up this mess." He stomped out of the living room and into the downstairs bathroom, slamming the door.

Ricky walked upstairs feeling triumphant, but also bewildered. That was not the trick he'd been practicing. He felt possessed, as if a spirit had entered his body and taken over. It unsettled him, but he had to admit that he also loved it. This was something extraordinary, something more than just an illusion or an effect.

He stood at the top of the stairs and looked down at his mother picking up the cards. Through a small window on the other side of the upstairs hallway, he saw the almost-full moon lighting up the front yard. He shook his head and went into his room.

Ever since Ricky saw a magician perform at a friend's birthday party two years ago, he was enthralled. He loved everything about it – the patter, the effortless glide of the hands, the misdirection, the miraculous effects. He saved up and went to a magic shop in the city, got a few books and some props, and practiced obsessively. He went back to the shop many times and got to know the proprietor, Mr. Graffeo, who greeted Ricky each time by name and took his time explaining the history of the various illusions, the basics of performance, the techniques by which to achieve maximum effect. Ricky now had dozens of tricks he was working on. He didn't know anyone at school who was as fascinated by magic as he was, and he was sure this would become his unique skill, the thing that made him special, worthy of other's admiration and esteem. At first, he only showed the tricks to his best friend David, but other classmates started wandering over, and his audiences grew until there could be as many as twenty who gathered to watch his lunchtime performances. Some were older kids who would never otherwise be seen with Ricky, and there was a girl that Ricky had a crush on but was too shy to speak to.

One day, Ricky was doing a series of coin tricks in the cafeteria when he saw Axel Martin approaching from across the room. Ricky hated Axel Martin. He was a widely-feared bully, capable of great cruelty, without provocation or remorse. One day last year, for no apparent reason, he slapped Ricky in the back of the head as he passed him in the hallway. When Ricky said, "Hey, what was that for?" Axel grabbed him by the front of his shirt and threw him up against the lockers. If David hadn't alerted a teacher in a nearby classroom, Ricky might have taken a real beating. Since then, Ricky kept his distance, and walked in the opposite direction whenever he saw Axel coming.

Seeing him now, walking toward them in his leather jacket and ripped jeans, it could mean only one thing – Axel was going to pick someone out of the group, rough them up, and take their money. Ricky stiffened and stopped in the middle of the trick he was performing for fear of messing up.

Axel pushed one of the kids aside and said, "What's going on here at the nerd convention?"

"Ricky's doing magic tricks," said David in a nervous rush of words. "You should check it out."

Ricky was feeling a little feisty after last night's incident with his father, so he thought he might be able to distract Axel with a coin trick. "Axel," he said, his voice trembling a bit. "Watch this." He held a quarter in one hand, then grabbed it with his other hand and closed his fingers around it. He shook his fist as if he was about to roll a pair of dice, then held it out in front of Axel. "Blow on it," he said.

"Blow me," said Axel, scowling. David stifled a laugh, and the girl Ricky has a crush on gasped. Ricky wasn't sure if she was offended by Axel's vulgarity or fearful on Ricky's behalf about what Axel might do.

"Okay, watch," Ricky said. He opened his hand and it was empty. Ricky heard a few oohs and aahs as he kept his eyes on Axel. There was a whistling sound from across the room; suddenly a quarter came flying out of nowhere and hit Axel full force on the forehead.

"Ouch!" Axel screamed, and everyone ran. "You're dead, Magic Boy!" he yelled as Ricky ducked out a side door.

Two periods later, when Ricky and David sat next to each other in history class, David leaned over and whispered, "Are you crazy?! Axel Martin's going to kill you. But ... that was awesome! How'd you do it?"

"Magicians never tell," Ricky whispered back. But just like that night with his father, he really had no idea.

Over the next week, Ricky practiced his magic tricks with a new sense of urgency. Cards, coins, scarves, a rope that would reattach after he cut it with scissors, balls that would disappear and reappear, metal rings that would pass through each other. He did the tricks alone in his room, watching himself in the mirror, and even though he was getting really good, it wasn't as much fun without an audience, without someone to fool, someone to amaze. He somehow understood that he had to keep practicing until he was perfect – there could be no slip-ups – if he wanted the real magic like the card in his father's mouth or the quarter that beaned Axel Martin to continue to happen. And although he felt intoxicated by these new magic powers, he was also unnerved by how unpredictable and beyond his control they were.

"Ricky! Dinner!" his mother called from downstairs.

"Coming." He took one last look in the mirror. With a snap of his wrists, he made the cards he had fanned in each hand disappear. He hung his jacket on a hook in the closet and sauntered downstairs with a big smile.

A few days after the incident in the cafeteria, Ricky was standing with David and a few others in front of the school, waiting for the afternoon bus. When he saw Axel Martin coming toward them, he braced for a confrontation.

Axel stepped up to him and said, "I've been looking for

you, Magic Boy. And I owe you this." He reared back and punched Ricky in the face. Ricky felt a jolt of pain through his whole body. He had never been punched like that before. A few of Axel's posse laughed. Ricky's friends were too intimidated to say anything, and stood in petrified silence.

Ricky tasted the blood in his mouth. He turned toward the school building and saw his reflection in one of the windows. A bruise was forming where he'd been hit, and a stream of blood ran down his chin. He turned and faced Axel. He saw the small scar on Axel's forehead from the coin trick in the cafeteria. He also noticed, for the first time, that Axel was about the same height as he was. Ricky had always imagined him much taller.

Ricky felt something stir in his chest. "That which you have done I declare undone. That which you do I return unto you!" He had no idea where these words came from, and his voice sounded odd, otherworldly. He drew his hand across his face and Axel fell back as if he'd been struck.

Everyone looked at Ricky. "The blood is gone," someone yelled. Ricky looked at his reflection again and there was no blood or bruise. Axel's face was covered with blood and a big purple welt had raised on his cheek. Ricky hadn't touched him.

"Wow," said David. "That was insane!"

"How'd he do that?" one of Axel's crew called out. Axel spun around and slapped him for the offense of being impressed.

Ricky turned and walked away. Even though his body was buzzing, he tried to appear calm as he wondered what was happening to him. But he knew two things. This was real magic, and it was thrilling.

Ricky had always imagined that his magic tricks would be the special talent that drew people to him, but after the run-in with Axel, the opposite was happening. Walking through the halls of the school, he saw the other students pointing at him and whispering. They would step aside and let him pass or duck around a corner to avoid him. It was as if they were afraid of him, like he was some kind of freak. One day in English class, even the girl he had a crush on scurried away when he finally worked up the courage to approach her so he could introduce himself.

The only person who stuck by him was David, who remained a loyal sidekick, always encouraging and enthusiastic. Ricky asked David what people were saying about him, and after hesitating, David said, "They see the surprise in your face. I see it too. They think the tricks are out of your control, and they're afraid they might get hurt."

Even with David's support, Ricky felt isolated and alone, and he still didn't quite understand what was happening, or why. He decided to ask the one person he thought would understand, and maybe offer some advice – Mr. Graffeo from the magic shop.

"Hello, Ricky," Graffeo said with a big smile. "It's good to see you again. How have you been?" He looked performance-ready as always – perfectly fitted black suit, this time with a red carnation in the lapel, white shirt, red bow tie, hair slicked back, pencil moustache.

"Good and bad, I guess," said Ricky. "I need your help."

"My pleasure, of course. What is it?" Graffeo stepped out from behind the counter.

"I'm getting really good," said Ricky. "Maybe too good."

"No such thing, young man. No such thing."

Ricky shifted his weight back and forth, and looked at the floor. "The tricks go way beyond the effects that I practice. Things happen ... I don't even know how to describe it."

"That's a good thing, Ricky. That means you've gone on to the next level, which not everyone can do. You're crossing over into real magic. It's the difference between being an illusionist and a conjurer."

"What does that even mean, Mr. Graffeo? I don't understand."

"You will in time. But don't you find it exhilarating?"

"Yes, I guess. But these tricks are just illusions and I know the secrets behind them, or what's supposed to be behind them. And then ... things happen. Coins fly out of nowhere. I even had a folded card appear in my father's *mouth*. I can't explain it. It's like I'm not even the one doing it." Ricky wondered if he sounded crazy.

Graffeo smiled and clapped Ricky on the shoulder. "Let's go in the back. I want to show you something."

They walked through a door behind the counter into a dimly lit room crowded with all kinds of props and equipment. Ricky thought it smelled a little like a barn, and then he noticed against the back wall a row of cages with birds, rabbits, snakes, and a large iguana. "I see you've noticed my assistants," Mr. Graffeo said. "Want to hold one?"

Before Ricky could answer, Graffeo took a metal box off a nearby table, showed Ricky that it was empty, then spun it around, reached inside, and pulled out an iguana. He put it on Ricky's shoulders. Ricky looked at the cage in the back; the iguana that had been there seconds before was gone.

"His name is Juan," Graffeo said, smiling broadly. "Juan the Iguana. He's from Mexico. But you look a little uncomfortable. Here." Graffeo produced a red silk scarf from nowhere and draped it over Ricky's head and shoulders. Ricky heard a loud *whoosh*. Graffeo withdrew the scarf and Juan was gone. Ricky looked back at the cage and there he was.

"Juan and I have been practicing teleportation for a few weeks, and I think we've finally got it."

Ricky didn't know what to say. Graffeo's trick was incredible, but that's not why he was here. "Mr. Graffeo, can you help me? I need my tricks to be more ... I don't know ... under control."

"No, no, my friend. At this stage, you need to surrender yourself to these new powers, feel the energy surging through you, and discover what magic – real magic – can do." Graffeo stared wistfully off to the side for a moment. He looked back at Ricky. "I think I know what might help." He motioned with one hand, and a deck of cards appeared. He motioned with the other hand and produced a few small sheets of clear plastic. He handed the deck to Ricky. "These cards have some powers of their own that will go well with what you're experiencing. Put them in your pocket for now and hold out your hands."

Ricky did as he was told. Graffeo laid a sheet of the clear plastic in each palm. The plastic wrapped around Ricky's hands and seemed to melt into them.

"These plastic sheets enable you to create one of my favorite effects," Graffeo said. "Keep your palm up and do this." Graffeo motioned as if tossing something aside. When Ricky copied the gesture, a small flame appeared in his hand. Ricky was startled at first, then became aware that he felt no burning sensation.

"Now toss the flame into your other hand as if it were a tennis ball." Again, Ricky complied, and the flame jumped from one hand to the other. Ricky smiled, then tossed the flame back and forth several more times.

"Very good. I see you've got the hang of it. I never understood the admonition about not playing with fire." Graffeo laughed. "Now throw the flame at that curtain." Ricky faced a dark red curtain hanging from a metal rod on the ceiling. He made a throwing motion. The curtain burst into flames, and in seconds, all that was left was a wisp of smoke. With the curtain gone, a large sign was revealed. "Congratulations, Ricky," it read in elaborate script. "You are now ready!"

Graffeo stuffed the remaining plastic sheets into Ricky's shirt pocket and said, "You are one of the fortunate ones, one of the gifted ones who can take things beyond mere tricks, mere illusions. As a *conjurer*, you now have a responsibility to embrace this power. The power of magic!" He shook Ricky's hand, then walked him back into the shop and out the door. Ricky tried to make sense of it all – power and responsibility, illusion and conjuring, magic tricks and real magic. He suspected there was more to it, and that Graffeo wasn't telling him everything.

The next morning at school, Ricky was excited to tell David about Graffeo and the magic shop. David wasn't at his locker, and he wasn't in first period math class. Ricky walked into the cafeteria for his lunch period and scanned the room. Still no David. He took out the deck of cards Graffeo had given him and began shuffling, thinking he might attract a small audience. After a group of students looked over then looked away, he put the cards back in his pocket, got his lunch, and sat alone at a table against the back wall.

Two girls came running toward him. Ricky recognized them as part of his lunchtime audience, but he didn't know their names.

"Ricky! You've got to come outside," one said, panting.

Ricky looked up at them. "Why? What's going on?" He felt embarrassed that he sounded just like his father – annoyed, put upon, as if he couldn't be bothered.

"It's David!" the other one said. "Axel Martin and his disgusting goony friends dragged him outside. They've got him under the bleachers."

Ricky dumped his uneaten lunch into a nearby waste bin, and ran out of the building and around to the back of the school where the ball fields were.

As he approached the bleachers, he saw Axel Martin and his posse of idiots. They had David tied to the bleachers' metal supports and they were taking turns punching him in the stomach. There were no teachers anywhere in sight.

Ricky stood about twenty feet away. "Knock it off, Axel! That's enough!" When they all turned toward him, Ricky snapped his fingers and the ropes that bound David fell away.

David tried to run, but Axel grabbed him by the arm. "Look who's here! Magic Boy to the rescue, right on schedule. If you want your friend, come and get him."

On any other day, Ricky would have been scared, or nervous, or tongue-tied. But today he felt powerful. And angry! It was if he were possessed, just like that first night with his parents and the card trick, but even more so. "You have no idea what you're dealing with, Axel." He produced Graffeo's deck of cards. "Pick a card."

"You've got to be kidding!" Axel said.

"Never mind. I'll pick it for you. How about this one?" He pulled a card from the deck. "Well what do you know, it's a club. The jack of clubs." Ricky flicked it at Axel. The card whistled through the air and hit Axel right in the eye, knocking him back a step.

Axel yelped and put his hand to his face. He grabbed David's arm tighter. "That's it. You're dead. I'm gonna kill both of you!"

Ricky held his hands out, snapped his wrists, and two small flames appeared in his palms. "Last chance, Axel. Let him go."

"Yeah, right!" Axel snarled.

"Wrong answer," Ricky said calmly. He felt electrified.

Ricky threw the fire in Axel's direction. In seconds, the entire bleachers went up in flames. The posse scattered, leaving only Axel and David.

Ricky was alarmed at the sight of the huge fire, but couldn't stop himself. His hands seemed to be moving on their own. "Okay Axel. This one's for you." He produced another ball of flame and threw it. Axel Martin ignited instantly and was consumed by fire in the blink of an eye. There was a puff of gray smoke, and a small pile of ash dropped to the ground where

Axel had been standing.

Ricky saw David lying on the ground nearby. He ran to him and dragged him away from the heat of the bleacher fire. He saw that David's arm and the side of his face were badly burned. Ricky wiped David's sweat-soaked hair off his forehead. "Are you okay?" He started to feel a little sick.

"Yes, Ricky, I'm fine," David said, then he broke into a coughing fit that lasted a few seconds. When the coughing subsided, he said, "I'm okay. *Really*. Thanks for being such a good friend." He coughed twice more, then passed out.

Ricky heard the sirens, then saw the flashing lights. Someone must have called. Firemen with hoses were running to put out the fire, and an ambulance pulled off the road, onto the grass, and right up to where he and David were. The EMTs put David on a stretcher and loaded him in. Ricky watched them drive away, then turned and walked slowly back into the school through the crowd of students and teachers who stepped aside to let him pass.

When Ricky was questioned by school officials and by the police, he played dumb, and recounted what happened in a manner that confirmed their suspicions that Axel Martin was responsible for the fire. Later, Ricky learned that Axel had been abandoned by his parents many years ago and lived in a group foster home where he regularly terrorized the other children and was repeatedly in trouble with the police. He was despised, resented, or feared by everyone who knew him. The host family and the state agencies did nothing to follow-up or investigate, and in spite of their public expressions of regret, were happy to be done with him.

The next day, Ricky went back to the magic shop, and was surprised to see a sign in the window that read, "Commercial space, available for lease." A few doors down, he saw Mr. Graffeo loading boxes into a rental truck. Ricky walked up to him and said, "Mr. Graffeo, what's going on? Where are you going?"

"Hello, Ricky. It's time for me to move on, that's all. I'm glad you're here so I could say goodbye."

"But why, Mr. Graffeo? Why do you have to go?"

"You did good, Ricky," Graffeo said, ignoring the question. "I heard all about what happened at school. You stood up to a bully, and I'm proud of you."

"Proud of me?!" Ricky yelled. "For what?! I just wanted to be special, to be liked. I used to love magic. I *still* love magic, but ... I didn't want this! Because of you, all the other kids avoid me ... 'cause they're afraid of me!"

Graffeo smiled. "I know it's confusing. Just give it time. Remember what I said about the difference between an illusionist and a conjurer? You have a gift. I could sense it the first time you came into the shop, and I am grateful to have been there to help you experience your gift, to find your power. You're still young, and you still have a young man's intensity of feeling, which is both a blessing and a curse. Anger, longing, joy, contempt, fear, love. As you learn to control these emotions, so too will your newfound powers come under your control. And then, there will be no limit to what you can achieve!"

"Yeah, but look what I've *achieved* so far. On top of everything else, you've made me a murderer! I didn't like Axel Martin, but that doesn't mean I want to kill him!"

"Don't look at it that way, Ricky. You've rid the world of evil. A tiny fraction of the evil in the world, but still. Learn from this. From now on, it's up to you to decide what you want to do, what you want to accomplish, with your magic powers." He put his hand on Ricky's shoulder. "Goodbye, Ricky. It's been an honor."

Ricky was speechless. Graffeo loaded the last box in and drove away. Ricky watched the truck pull to a stop sign. Graffeo stuck his arm out the window, waved back at Ricky, then snapped his fingers. There was a small flash of light and the truck vanished.

Ricky wandered the streets for a few hours before he went home, trying to make sense of what Graffeo had said. When he finally walked in his front door, he heard his mother call from the kitchen, "Oh, there you are! Wash up, dinner's almost ready."

"Okay," said Ricky, feeling exhausted. "I'll be down in a minute."

He grabbed a garbage bag from the hall closet and went up to his room. He gathered all his magic props and paraphernalia – the cards, the coins, the scarves, the ropes, the balls, the metal rings, the magic wand … even his top hat and his red bow tie, and put them in the bag. He walked down the back stairs and put the bag in a trash can. He pressed the last sheet of Mr. Graffeo's clear plastic into his palm and summoned a small ball of fire. He looked down into the trash can, then changed his mind. He threw the fire at a small pile of leaves that ignited, burned for a few seconds, then died out. Ricky retrieved the garbage bag and took it back into the house. He went up to his room and stuffed it into the back corner of his closet. He joined his parents at the dinner table and ate his meat loaf, broccoli, and mashed potatoes in silence.

# Igniting Moons, for You
## by Herma S.Y. Li

The last body of the Moons I kept
has burnt down to its skeleton.
The flames, they used to dance like quicksilver.
Like poisoned meteors. Like adrenalized vision.
The celestial innards, once were blazing
with sacrificial light,
are now pieces of broken paleness
to warm us through one last night.

So I have to sin for you, to hunt down Moons again,
grasp at midnight air and come back with glowing scars on my hand.

To tear through the skin of what is so pure, it makes you seem unclean,
drag the insides apart then bleed out nonflammable dreams----
uneven, jagged as your tragedy.
While it draws blood with the slightest touch, like my destiny
reflected a thousand times in a maze of mirrors.
Burning darkness along with truth to forget that
life is a compound of flaws and errors:

Everyone laughs, everyone cries.
(Birthday candles, braces, graduation, hard work, heavy safe)
Everyone lies, everyone dies.
(Wedding dresses, denture, retirement, hollow life, lonely grave)

So when the time comes, I bid you forget the wrongs I've done.
Including me killing Moons.
Leave me reasons to be missed, not many, some.
And I shall continue the crime that makes lights bloom.

# The Lion's Gate
## by Caroline Reddy

It's time to resurrect my light
so that I can rewire a new path
as I rewind these neuron memories
and liberate
the yellow-green speckles
from the bloated fish,
that washed up on the beach years ago.

Even if I enter the Lion's gate
the amber tapestry painted
across the August beams
still might embrace the salty residue
that trapped me in a loop for years.

The sunflowers
can circle around the smiling sun
as the illusions begin to fade from my heart.

The veil between the dimensions is thin
ever since I began to believe
and I have waited so long
for the mind to awaken
to the way
so that the magician is more than a
mere silhouette in the moonrise.

I close my eyes and bask in the orbs
that appear in the golden hall
allowing myself to chant
the spell-casting secrets from within.

I unleash my shield and reforge my sword
to spark an inner flame
to prepare me for the portal
as Leo and Sirion align with Orion's belt.

# DEEP PERK
# DOVE
# STOCK

*Shakespeare*

# Shakespeare in Winter
## by Lynette G. Esposito

the aching snowflakes
cling like cold butterflies
to the black fingers
of dark barren trees
reaching upward
to the storm-driven sky
with no recourse
but to bear
the onslaught of
the storm
and the
wind's winter teeth...
a tempest.

# My Cousin Shakespeare Said
## by Lynette G. Esposito

Rules of the game,
Pray thee know,
Are many in the beginning
And few when you go.

Take up thy May flowers
And scatter them wide
For your funeral is coming
After you've died.

And those who come
to pay the last goodbye
with sorrow in their hearts
and tears in their eye
should be as many as the petals
you shared in your prime
that bless your passing
with sweet memory of your time.

# There's No Place Like Homophobia

by Timothy Arliss OBrien

My villain origin story

I get mostly the same response when I tell people where I'm from: Oklahoma.
Now to get you to imagine…
I'm a loud effeminate gay that dresses in more pastels and neons than an acid trip.
And I don't take kindly to others telling me how to act and what to do.
I've had my personality compared to the anti-hero and my husband occasionally jokes about me being a demon-twink. (But that is mostly when we are shopping and I don't get my way.)

Point blank, I'm a fairy, a poof, a homosexual, a faggot.
I'm queer.
And by now you're thinking "his home was middle America? The Bible Belt? Yikes."

Yes. That's the response I usually get.

As I'm writing this the news is swamped with questions on what could happen to the future of Lawrence v. Texas, and Obergefell v. Hodges, since Roe v. Wade was just overturned.

I remember being in high school in 2004 when the Oklahoma House of Representatives, by a vote of 92 to 4, approved a constitutional ban on same-sex marriage. And then later in the year when Oklahoma voters approved Oklahoma Question 711, a constitutional amendment which banned same-sex marriage.

I also remember living in Portland and encountering the epiphanous day of the ruling of Obergefell v. Hodges while I was working at the county building, and the amount of celebration and joy we all felt. We could finally get married to the love of my life.

So how does home fit into that kind of picture?
It's difficult. I want to be proud of where I grew up but even with the disgrace and shame from the culture I grew up with I do have fond memories of my childhood.

But that does not aid or even come close to resolve the terror and trauma I as a queer person experienced growing up in the culture.
The bullies roughed me up because I acted too much like the girls. The threats of violence and vile homophobic epitaphs screamed at me by strangers.
"You're gonna have to move to somewhere like Cali or San Fran if you want to live like that."
It's disgusting that children should experience that from the age of five onward.

See not only are these things important to me as someone that is queer, but also because I'm a survivor of years of electroshock ex-gay therapy.
The amount of shame and self hatred that these religious institutions forcibly embed in us is worse than evil.
And seeing how my own humanity is protected by the law comparatively from Oklahoma to Oregon, is depressing.

As I am writing this, twenty of the states ban conversion therapy for minors, including Oregon. And 22 states have no state law or policy, including Oklahoma.
In fact the Movement Advancement Project tracks over fifty different LGBTQ related laws and policies and the categories of laws covered by their policy tally include: Relationship & Parental Recognition, Nondiscrimination, Religious Exemptions, LGBTQ Youth, Health Care, Criminal Justice, and Identity Documents.
Oregon falls in one of the highest tallys in the top fifteen. While Oklahoma has received a negative tally being actively harmful for LGBTQ rights with eight other states.
I urge you to visit lgbtmap.org to understand what we are dealing with.

I will never be safe and able to thrive where I grew up.

I wish I could sit here and tell you I am excited when I get on the plane to Oklahoma for a visit back to family. But with the state of the churches encroaching on our personal rights, freedom of expression, and bodily autonomy, I dread traveling to any place with such a draconian culture.

The culture shock alone is enough to kill you.

Home has become somewhere I've had to search for and build for myself over years. It's become the nude beach where I can be one with nature and contemplate the deepest quandaries of my psyche. It has become my husband and our friends. And all the late nights and rowdy New Year's Eve parties that left me hungover for weeks.

Home has become the gay bars where I cry at the overwhelming power, beauty, and courage of some of my favorite drag queens. And the momentous longing I get for the pride parade every year that I get to march in and celebrate the fact that god made me perfect.

Of course it's also my apartment where I express myself in my recording studio and publishing house with my angry little kitten.
Home is what we make it.
But the issue at hand is that so many of us queer people are at a disadvantage without the resources to build a life for ourselves to not only thrive, but to merely survive.

I hope that you are able to find and build that safety and freedom for yourself.

We must scream our queer joy loudly and give our selves permission to not only take up space in this world, but celebrate that we exist.

# Mama's Little Angel
## by Z.B. Wagman

"*My little angel.*" It was what my mama called me since before I could remember. She said that I was the most beautiful child to ever exist--her "*gift from God.*" According to her, when I was born the nurses couldn't look away. They said that I was the most beautiful baby they had ever seen. A mother's exaggeration. No one ever told me I was beautiful.

Growing up, the other children avoided me as if they thought I had some disease. My mother said that they were just jealous. That they wished they were as pretty as me. That they wished they could be special. But she didn't see the way they laughed. She didn't hear the mockery in their voice when they called me a freak.

The older I got, the more I receded inward. Wherever I went, I could feel their eyes scrutinizing every inch of me. And not just from the kids. Even my teachers, when they thought I wasn't watching, would allow their gaze to linger over me. One of them even told my mother that I was a distraction. He asked if there was something I could do to "cover up."

That's when I started to bind. It was my idea, my mother didn't want me to. She would say things like, "You have to love yourself." But life was so much easier when I could feel the wrapping biting into my chest. With a big sweatshirt on, nobody could tell that I stood out. It was easier to love the me that slipped unnoticed into the crowd.

I went to a public high school across town where nobody knew my name. Nobody cared. Nobody noticed the girl in the back of the class with the too-large hoodie. It was easy. And even though nobody talked to me, for once I was rid of the stares. It was freeing. For the first time in my life I felt like I could be me.

And then I met Paul. He was the other loner who sat at

the back of art class. He was ignored by everyone else, but it seemed that he liked it that way. When they called him a freak, he would smile and thank them. "Freaks run this world," he would say. And even though the others would still cackle with derision, Paul's smile wouldn't falter. It took me weeks to pluck up the courage to talk to him. It had been a long time since I had sought contact. I shouldn't have worried.

"I like your painting. You've got good perspective."

"Thanks. Gabby, right? You're the one who transferred from Southside."

Though awkward at first, Paul and I became close friends. Soon we were spending every day together. I thought that I had been happy when everyone ignored me. But now I knew that I had been lying to myself. Paul listened when I talked. We argued, we fought, and for the first time ever I felt like I was alive. That was when I made my mistake.

The first time I showed myself to a boy, a shiver that worked its way down my spine and through my extremities. My hands shook as I began to lift my sweater. When it came over my head, blocking my view, I heard Paul gasp. And then I was standing there, letting him look--letting him touch--as the bindings slipped to the floor. He had a way of making me feel like I mattered. Like I really was special. But the next day at school, everything had changed.

"I heard you fly, guuurl."

"I knew you was keeping something hidden."

"I'll show you mine if you show me yours."

Everyone knew. The comments, the stares, the names all came pouring back. I couldn't make it down the hallway without heads turning and whispers following in my wake. And Paul was the center of it all. His smile, the same one he had flashed in the faces of our bullies, now joined with theirs.

My mama tried to comfort me. But I didn't want to hear how "boys are assholes" or that "it will all get better soon." Her crooning about how special I was nauseated me. All I wanted to do was cry. But Paul's leering face kept swimming up through my tears. I could still remember his hands running across my skin. And the way his breath caught as the binding fell to the floor. I needed to be rid of him. I needed to be rid of them all.

It was easy sitting through class, knowing what was coming. I almost didn't notice the peering eyes or the names whispered in the halls. Even Paul, coming face to face with his mocking smile wasn't enough to shake me.

"What's up birdie?" His gleeful tone rang across the courtyard.

"Paul."

"Come over later and we can get high."

"Whatever."

"Come on. You busy? What's a little freak like you busy with anyway?"

"Freaks run this world, Paul."

When the last buzzer rang, I made my way up to the roof. Far below I could see the bullshit of our everyday life. The fleeting romances and vapid cliques. I pulled off my hoodie and climbed onto the ledge. It was the easiest climb I had ever made. I already felt free. I could hear shouts and jeering drifting up from below but, whether or not they were for me I did not know. I closed my eyes, drowning out the clamor below. A light spring wind brushed against my cheek. It was calling me. Egging me on. It was all the encouragement I needed. I took that step.

The wind whistles in my ears. For a moment I heard shouting from the crowd as the pavement rushed up to greet me.

Then I opened my wings.

# BB Keeping
## by Desiree Ducharme

BB was a beekeeper. An advocate of the apiary arts. He wrote several tomes on the subject. It was not how he made a living, but how he loved living. Everyone called him "BB." BB had six sons. Each of BB's sons, known as GBs, had six sons, known as FBs. And each one of the FBs had six sons. Well, almost. She should have been GG216. To be fair, everyone still called her GG216. Except BB. BB called her QB. She was the only one of his progeny interested in beekeeping. The rest of them were only interested in building and buying things.

BB was an ancient man by the time QB was born. He spent his days walking away from the buildings and barns and boardwalks that his sons and grandsons and great-grandsons were constantly adding to the property. They filled them with bobbles and bling and when they broke they bought new ones. Each thing had a use. Each thing had a space. Each thing had a purpose. Each thing except BB and QB.

BB had fulfilled his purpose. He'd had his sons. He was no longer able to make money, to buy things, to fill space. He was surrounded by the noise of his success as they awaited his death.

QB was QB.

BB started with one hive. It actually started on the house. A gathering of wax and honey, of legs and wings, tucked under the eves. BB was a young man, not more than a child. He read a book on how to relocate the bees and built his first bee box, which he called BB1. He carried it through the orchard to a small rise, not really a hill, and placed the hive upon it. Then he walked away and let the bees be bees. Each year, the hive on the house appeared in spring. Each year, BB walked to a new part of the property and set up a new bee box.

The GBs built their homes in a circle between BB1 and BB's house (as the bees fly) with BB's house at the center. There was plenty of space for their structures. As their families grew, they added barns and garages, playhouses and storage sheds. They filled the space. They made money. They bought things and had sons.

The FBs built their homes around their fathers' houses between BB36 and BB1 (as the bees fly) with a GB's house at the center. They built multi-story homes for their broods and even more garages. They took out the orchard and filled it with trucks and wagons. They filled in the streams and paved the footpaths so GGs could drive ATVs between the GBs houses and their own.

GG216 was largely ignored, which suited her just fine. Her father (FB36) was too busy filling space with success and sons (GGs 210, 212-215) that he chose to ignore that GG216 was neither. They didn't talk to her, but about her, which is why she never talked back. Which suited them just fine.

"GG216 broke her window, again," reported GG213 after he broke the window in her room. GG216 listened.

"GG216 was late for dinner, again," reported GG210 after he'd forgotten to pick her up from BB's. GG216 listened.

"GG216 will need new clothes, again," reported FB36 as he pulled at the sleeves of her jacket trying to close the gap between cuff and wrist. A jacket that was once FB36's, then GG6,27,64,92,103,167… GG216 listened.

GG216 was dropped off at BB's house, every day, presumably to be watched by BB's nurse.
"I'm a nurse, not a nurse maid! You'll have to fend for yourself." At least he spoke directly to GG216 and GG216 listened. The nurse only made it to spring, when the bees arrived. Then he resigned without notice. Leaving the toddler and the old man to fend for themselves. Which was fine by them.

GG216 was 4 when she followed BB to the hives the first time. He was old and didn't move very fast. GG216 was a toddler and only moved fast unintentionally and generally in the direction of the ground. Their paces matched without effort. BB knew that hives were healthier when he talked to the bees. Which is perhaps why he began talking to GG216. Not really good with humans, BB talked about bees. GG216 listened.

In the fall, GG216 carried the hive in a bag while BB pulled the wagon with BB97. They passed the diminishing hum of the GBs' houses. Stopping briefly at BB1 still nestled on its rise, not really a hill. They followed the FB's asphalt path through what was once an orchard. BB told QB of the blossoms that once filled the air as GGs 200, 197, and 209 roared past them. Their wake left BB, QB, and the sack of bees coated with dust and anxiety. They reached the edge of FB12's circle and took the trail west into the woods.

"Bees prefer quiet." BB looked at his youngest great-grandchild. Just over four years old and silent as the bees in her hands. They were silent. The entire hive. "I think they prefer you, to be honest." QB had her first smile. "We need to walk for twenty more minutes. Bees don't like to be crowded." They passed BB53, BB60, BB88, and what BB told her was BB4. BB4 was a pile of sticks and mushrooms. Only BB53 had an active hive. The hive in her hands buzzed anxiously to their fellows. QB brought the bag to her chest and started to hum. BB listened. The bees settled. "All hives have a queen, just one." BB patted the top of her head, "When the queen leaves, the hive leaves." They installed BB97 near a hollow tree. BB called GG216 "QB" and QB listened.

BB and QB walked to the hives and back everyday. They collected honey in the wagon. QB pulled it until it became too heavy. Then BB pulled it home. That winter, GB1 died.

The general concern immediately following his death was what to do with his stuff. His sons (FB1,2,5,7,8 and 10) and brothers (GB2,3,4,5,and 6) gathered in the parlor of GB1's house and began to argue over a table filled with paper.

"We should split the estate six ways," FB1 began.
"He always wanted GG26 to have his laptop," FB2 interrupted.
"And for GG65 to have his car. The one that's paid off and still runs pretty good," FB10 added.
"GG1 was always his favorite and should get the boat," FB7 put in.
GB5 fuffed and shuffled in his chair. "The back gate is on my side and is a full six inches over the property line!" the elderly man exclaimed to the room in general.

GB2 banged his stick on the ancient hardwood several times. Hard enough to pop an old knot out. The buzz settled. "What does the will say?"

GB6 scoffed. "The will says what all our wills say." And it did. GB1's estate (any money and stuff) was split between his six sons with a special bequest of three items to each of his 36 grandsons, two items to each of his 6 brothers, and one item to each of his 179 nephews. They had to be able to carry it away on their own. The property was BB's and always had been. There was no provision for GG216. She was only 5. They didn't really think about it. QB didn't really think about it either, but she listened as BB read the will.

There was a great frenzy of activity at GB1's for several weeks that spring as the GBs, the FBs and the GGs (1-215) claimed (argued and fought over) their birthright. BB lead QB away from it. Something about watching them scurry and hurry through GB1's house made him ill at ease. He didn't want QB to see it. He had a twinge of something akin to regret. He liked to talk things through, especially now. (His memory not being what it once was.) QB listened.

"GB1 was my first child. My first son. He worked hard and built things and bought stuff and had sons of his own. There was a tree, where his barn is now. When he was a child, it was his favorite place." BB remembered the year they discovered a hive in this tree. It was the year GB1 left for college. BB left the hive and decided to offer GB1 the space for his home upon graduation. The first thing GB1 did was cut down the tree.

BB watched QB set up BB98 all the while gently humming. The sack already empty. The bees circling her in anticipation of their new home. "I never knew if he was happy. I never knew what brought him joy." QB took his ancient withered hand in her plump young one. She looked up at him and spoke her first words.

"He was a cranky bastard, BB. He was happiest when he was tearing things down, like BB4." She stuck a corner of honey filled wax in her mouth and sucked at it. BB laughed. Wondering if the moment really happened or if he was experiencing dementia. "What kind of tree was it?" a golden thread dripping from her chin.

"An oak, I think?"

His great grand-daughter smiled around her honeycomb. "Let's plant an acorn in the living room and poke a hole in the roof so it has a place to grow!" They laughed together. Poke a hole in the roof! What a ridiculous and delightful thought.

The crown of the oak tree rustled against the hole in the roof of GB1's old house. There was an active hive in the east corner of the porch, facing BB's house. QB and BB were delighted to find the hive there the year after GB1 passed. They did not relocate it. BB and QB hoped they would someday inhabit the tree. The last of the GBs (GB6) died during winter solstice. GG216 was not included in his will. Since none of the FBs or GGs inherited the property or houses, they left them alone and refused to maintain them. QB and BB planted trees in the living rooms and poked holes in their roofs. The day her father, brothers, uncles and cousins claimed their birthright, BB and QB gathered honey.

"BB, what will happen when FB36 dies?" Her hands covered in a thin layer of gold as she scraped honey from the screen of BB38.

"Same thing that happens when we all die. He'll be dead."

BB was too old to sugar-coat things.

"And the other GGs will clear out all his things?"

"I suppose."

"What will happen to me?"

"QB, your father is still quite young. You'll have a home of your own by the time he dies."

"How will I? I am like this hive." QB looked directly at her ancestor. "They tolerate me as long as I remain silent and sweet, and prefer when I am somewhere else."

BB, usually soothed by spending time with QB, was decidedly discomfited. The honey turned bitter in his mouth as she spoke. QB was quiet the rest of the day. They passed FB20's house as the ambulance pulled away. He'd had a heart attack while yelling at his lawyer over his share of GB3's estate. His six sons cleared the house of possessions, stripped it bare to the framework, within 24 hours. Then they left.

FB36 gathered his brood for a meeting. "I have inherited one sixth of GB6's estate. My estate will be split between the five of you. GG210, you will receive an additional stipend until GG216 marries." QB listened to her brothers' disappointment.

"Why does he get more!? How is that fair?" whined GG213

"What do I do with a girl?" GG210 wondered.

"Can we send her away now? Will a school take her?" GG212 suggested.

"Does he really need extra? GG216 spends all their time at BB's anyway…" GG214 speculated.

"GG216 is still alive? I thought she died, which is why GG213 took over her room." GG215 dismissed.

"Silence." FB36 shouted. "BB called me and asked that I make provisions for GG216. So I am."

"FB36, could I just have an equal share? One sixth, like all the other GGs?" QB asked reasonably.

"Don't be ridiculous. You will marry and have sons of your own. They will make money and build things. They will care for you." FB36 reassured her with a pat on the head. Her brothers each patted her head. QB listened to them squabble for several minutes. Then she was done listening.

"Split it five ways, I will care for myself." Then she left.

QB lived at BB's from then on. As the FBs died, the GGs stripped their homes to the framework and eventually left. In every husk, QB and BB planted seeds and established hives. There was plenty of room. The area around BB's grew silent. His sons were dead. His grandsons were dying. His great-grandsons were building and buying and having sons elsewhere. Which suited him just fine. On the last day of his exceptionally long life, he sat on his porch with QB and drank tea sweetened with honey. Cherry and plum blossoms floated lazily through the air.

"QB, what brings you joy?" BB knew hives were healthier when you talked to them.
"Bees," QB replied.

# XOXO, Candyman 2: a Creative Latin Composition Inspired by Bernard Rose's Candyman (1992)[1]

by Heather Hambley

### INTRA DIAETAM CDIV — NOCTE[2]

### MOVENS CUM HELENĀ

Helena[3] per diaetam discussam viam dat, lucillā[4] facis semitam illuminanti.

### INTRA BALNEUM — NOCTE

Helena armario medicamentorum pendenti in pariete se opponit[5]; quod[6] tarde aperit. In inani lumen luteum longe fulget. Animum[7] augens illa per foramen ascendit.

### INTRA CONCLAVE SANGUINEUM — NOCTE

Helena in primum cubiculum cruore aspersum repit. Paucae candelae lucem tenuem in solo spuunt. Illa per foramen in secundum conclave ascendit.

### EXTRA SECUNDUM FORAMEN — NOCTE

Helena ex ore imaginis Cuppediatoris emergit. Uncus desuper descendens in faciem Helenae tundit. Ea agiliter resalit videtque se ad unum uncorum lanii qui de tecto pendent offendisse[8]. Uncum de orbi eius tollit; nunc telum Helenae[9] est. Ad magnum foramen situm in extremo conclavis illa ambulat. Est inane atrum. Radius facis lucentis longinquum parietem tangere non potest. Sonus stillicidiorum[10] in lacunas labentium ex inani RESONAT. Quicquid ultra iacet, est vasta spelunca. Helena perscendit.

## INTRA CUBILE[11] CUPPEDIATORIS — NOCTE

Helena in pariete haerens per conclave atrum it[12]. Lucilla seriem picturarum muralium illuminat, quae ritu imaginum iter sancti pingentium[13] praebent[14]:

Cuppediator per oppidum a grassatoribus feris agitatur. Vulgus spectat, quorum[15] nemo misero opem fert.

Cuppediator denudatur atque manus serrā praeciditur.

Denique Cuppediator in saxis extensus examine apium ad mortem mordetur.[16]

De tenebris sonos ADSPIRATIONIS gravis tardaeque Helena audit. Luce obscurā[17] trans ingens conclave, multis parietibus ad cavernosum locum intra aedificium creandum[18] perfractis[19], quoddam Helena videt. Est cubile[20] de sanguineā lanii tabulā[21] factum; cui incubat supinus Cuppediator dormiens. Helena illum tacite aggreditur, vibrans uncum et parata percutere.

Propius propiusque it, auscultans constantem Cuppediatoris ADSPIRATIONEM et orans ne ille expergiscatur[22]. Helena iam est tam propinqua ut uncum in caput eius condere[23] possit[24]. Bracchium tollit.

Videmus faciem Cuppediatoris, oculis apertis[25].

CUPPEDIATOR (leniter): Helena…

Illa uncum in cervicem condit[26]. Cuppediator vix tergiversatur atque eximit telum sicut spinam.

CUPPEDIATOR (voce iam summissā): Helena…

Subito sedet recte rapitque illam. Uncus e manu Helenae cadit. Oculi Cuppediatoris desiderio[27] implentur.

CUPPEDIATOR: Venisti ad me. Deposueram spem, at animus meus gaudio impletur. Mea eris[28]?

Uncum suum[29] in tergo ponit, eleganter complectens Helenam. Saltare eam cogit.

CUPPEDIATOR: …in aeternum?

Saltant per conclave, sicut solo supernatant. Cum saltant, Cuppediator unco tergum Helenae tarde mulcet. Uncus cervicem palpat — primo leniter, deinde tali cum pressu[30] ut cutem rubicundam incidat[31]. Helena in bracchiis illius tremit.

CUPPEDIATOR: Victima mea sis[32].

HELENA: Non…desiste…obsecro…

CUPPEDIATOR: Pacti sumus.[33]

HELENA: Timida sum.

CUPPEDATIOR: Timesne dolorem, an quid ultra iaceat[34]?

HELENA: Utraque…

CUPPEDIATOR: Dolorem fore[35] dulcissimum iuro…quod attinet ad[36] infinitum[37] ipsum…in morte stabilitas nobis[38] non est. Fama[39] nostra in centum parietibus et decem milia oribus pingetur. Si quis[40] de nobis iterum dubitet, dulcedine[41] invocari[42] semper possumus[43].

*Special thanks to Allie Pohler.*

---

[1] This composition is primarily inspired by Bernard Rose's original screenplay for *Candyman* (1992). I chose this section because it focuses on the horror of Candyman's origins, as well as the tragic love story playing out between Candyman and Helen. The screenplay naturally differs from the movie in certain details and dialogue, but I tried to incorporate moments and observations from the movie throughout my translation.

[2] Alright, let's set the mood! I translated most of this comp to Philip Glass's haunting score *The Music of Candyman*. The whole album is a revelation and worth listening to, but this section picks up at "Return to Cabrini."

[3] I placed *Helena* first in these initial scenes to reflect the audience's POV as she enters Candyman's lair, which focuses on Helen looking around (as opposed to what she sees); we shift to her POV when she focuses on the murals depicting Candyman's death.

[4] Helen uses a penlight in the movie, presumably from the nurse's uniform that she stole in her escape from the psychiatric hospital. I wanted to form my own diminutive noun from *lux*, 'light' to reflect the penlight's small and focused beam, so I added the diminutive suffix *-illa* to *lux*'s base *luc-*, to mean 'a little light' (Allen & Greenough 243).

⁵   *Se opponere*, 'to face, confront' here because Helen is both literally facing the medicine cabinet as well as figuratively facing her fears, as she now knows what (and who) lies behind the cabinet. The verb can also have adversarial connotations, so I wanted to foreshadow Helen's confrontation with Candyman.
⁶   *quod*: connecting relative with *armarium*
⁷   I had originally wanted to use *virtus*, which, like *animus*, can be translated as 'courage,' but additionally as 'manliness' and 'military excellence.' It's a term typically applied to male heroes, so I thought it could be fun to play with gender here. However, my editor explained that *virtus* is often an external quality, demonstrated through military prowess and displays of masculinity; *animus*, on the other hand, reflects a courage that comes from within, which I think better describes what we see from Helen. I like how her relationship with fear and courage evolve throughout the movie. Her first time to Cabrini-Green, she walks in fearlessly (and, I'd argue, foolishly) and even taunts Bernadette for exercising reasonable caution. She isn't scared by the stories of Candyman because she doesn't believe in him. Compare this to Helen's final visit to Cabrini-Green, after she's experienced the real and deadly power of Candyman; her fear is palpable in this scene, but she's nevertheless resolved to save baby Anthony and enters, knowing that she may not come out alive.
⁸   *se... offendisse*: indirect statement
⁹   dative of possession
¹⁰  I used the noun *cubile* for Candyman's lair because it can indeed mean 'lair, den', but it also often translates to 'marriage bed' (fun fact: Vergil even uses *cubile* for 'hive of bees'! cf. Verg. *Georgics*, 4.243). I wanted to play with this double-meaning in light of Candyman's pursuit of and desire for Helen. I like reading this scene as something of a homecoming for Helen too.
¹¹  My editor and I had a hilarious time puzzling over how to translate 'to move' intransitively because *movēre* is primarily a transitive verb — it's *ire*, 'to go!' *Picard facepalm*
¹²  *ritu imaginum iter sancti pingentium*: 'in the manner of paintings depicting the journey of a saint'; *imaginum* refers back to the Roman death masks worn in public funerals to honor the dead and reanimate their ancestors with their likenesses depicted in wax, cf. my first comp *XOXO, Candyman: a Creative Latin Composition Inspired by Clive Barker's "The Forbidden."* I also like the connection to Candyman's past life as an artist (this detail was not in Rose's original backstory for Candyman but was developed by Tony Todd). I used *iter* to describe Candyman's passage through life (and death), as well as to echo Helen's journey through Candyman's lair and his story.
¹³  The true horror of *Candyman* — the lynching of Candyman. I switch to staccato sentences in the indicative here to keep the images of Candyman's capture, torture, and death vivid and real.
¹⁴  antecedent is the collective noun *vulgus*
¹⁵  The movie regrettably doesn't show a painting of Candyman being stung to death by bees. The screenplay doesn't go into much detail here, but we learned in Purcell's earlier speech that the men smashed the hives of a nearby apiary and rubbed stolen honeycomb on Candyman's prone body.
¹⁶  I separated *luce obscurā* from the main verb *videt* to reflect the effort it takes Helen to make sense of the chaos and confusion of Candyman's lair.
¹⁷  *ad cavernosum locum... creandum*: I love me a purpose gerundive
¹⁸  *multis parietibus... perfractis*: ablative absolute
¹⁹  *cubile* again, here with its other meaning 'marriage bed'
²⁰  *de sanguineā... tabulā*: ablative of source or material

[21] *ne... expergiscatur*: negative indirect command

[22] I chose the verb *condere*, 'to thrust or strike in deep, to plunge,' which Ovid uses to describe Hecuba's fingers thrusting into Polymestor's eyes as she avenged her son's death; cf. Ovid, *Met.* 13.561). Ovid's *Metamorphoses* (specifically the story of Philomela) was my first foray into horror — I mean, does anyone write body horror as well as Ovid? — so I wanted to gesture to him here.

[23] *ut... possit*: result clause

[24] *oculis... apertis*: ablative absolute with an implied participle of esse (Allen & Greenough, 419a)

[25] Quick, impactful sentences reflect the action ramping up. It should feel easier to move through these sentences as we're focused on the back-and-forth between Candyman and Helen.

[26] I employed romantic and emotional language throughout this dialogue to express Candyman's twisted love for Helen (e.g., *desiderio, gaudio, complectens, mulcet*, etc.).

[27] I omitted the interrogative particle *-ne* per Allen & Greenough 332a, which says when *-ne* is omitted, "it is often doubtful whether the sentence is a question or an ironical statement." Can Helen truly deny Candyman's will here?

[28] I used the reflexive adjective with *uncum suum*, 'his own hook' here to distinguish between the two hooks in this scene: the butcher hook Helen is using as a weapon (which has just fallen out of her hand), and Candyman's hooked hand. I wanted to clarify that *uncus* from here on out refers to Candyman's *own* hook.

[29] *tali cum pressu*: ablative of manner

[30] *ut... incidat*: result clause

[31] jussive subjunctive

[32] i.e., Helen for baby Anthony

[33] *quid...iaceat*: indirect question

[34] *Dolorem... dulcissimam*: indirect statement with fore (the future infinitive of *esse*); *fore* is rare, but I wanted to capture that Candyman's speech and tone here feels formal and from another time.

[35] *quod attinet ad* (c. acc), 'as for'

[36] cf. Lucretius, *On the Nature of Things*, 2.1044-1045

[37] dative of possession

[38] Candyman is concerned with crafting their mythological narrative in the public eye. How will they be remembered? I also appreciate *fama*'s alternate translation of 'rumor,' as Candyman often refers to himself, "I am rumor," a line which also inspired the title of both my Candyman comps, cf. *Gossip Girl* ;)

[39] *quis = aliquis*; "After *si, nisi, num, ne*, all the *ali*-s fall away," as I was taught my first year of Latin and re-taught dozens of times thereafter, every time I translated as 'who.'

[40] I used both *dulcissimam* and *dulcedine* in Candyman's final speech of this section to recall Candyman's famous phrase, "Sweets to the sweet."

[41] The verb *invocare*, often used to invoke a god, emphasizes the ritualistic and otherworldly nature of calling Candyman. I also liked juxtaposing the idea of summoning Candyman (and now Helen) back 'with sweetness' (*dulcedine*) with the knowledge that their return will almost surely mean death for the invoker, as we see at the end of the movie with Trevor.

[42] *Si... dubitet... possumus*: mixed conditional with a future-less-vivid protasis and a present simple apodosis

# Glossary

**adspiratio**, -onis, f. *breathing*
**agito** (*1*), *to hunt, chase, pursue*
**animus**, -i, m. *courage, spirit; heart*
**aperio**, -ire, -ui, apertus, *to open*
**aspergo**, -ere, -ersi, -ersus, *to spatter*
**ater**, -tra, -trum, *black, dark*
**ausculto** (*1*), *to listen to*
**balneum**, -i, n. *bathroom*
**bracchium**, -i, n. *arm*
**cervix**, -icis, f. *neck*
**cogo**, -ere, coegi, coactus, *to force, compel*
**complector**, -i, -plexus, *dep. to clasp, embrace, grasp*
**conclave**, -is, n. *chamber, room*
**confringo**, -ere, -fregi, -fractus, *to smash*
**cruor**, -oris, m. *blood, bloodshed, gore*
**Cuppediator**, -oris, m. *Candyman*
**denudo** (*1*), *to lay bare, make naked, expose; to strip, plunder*
**depono**, -ere, -posui, positus, *to give up*
**diaeta**, -ae, f. *apartment*
**discutio**, -ere, -cussi, -cussus, *to shatter*
**dolor**, doloris, m. *pain*
**dulcedo**, -inis, f. *sweetness*
**eo**, ire, ii, itus, *to go, walk, move; advance*
**examen**, -inis, n. *swarm*
**eximo**, -ere, -emi, -emptus, *to take out, remove*
**expergiscor**, -i, -perrectus, *dep. to awake, be awakened*
**fax**, facis, f. *torch*
**ferus**, -a, -um, *savage, barbarous, cruel; wild*
**foramen**, -inis, n. *an opening, aperture, hole*
**fulgeo**, -ēre, fulsi, *to flash, glitter, gleam, shine*
**grassator**, -oris, m. *hoodlum, bully*
**haereo**, -ēre, haesi, haesurus, *to stick, cling*
**iaceo**, -ēre, -cui, -citus, *to lie (geographically)*
**imago**, -inis, f. *image, picture, portrait*
**impleo**, -ēre, -evi, -etus, *to fill up*
**inane**, -is, n. *an empty space, void*
**incido**, -ere, -cidi, -casus, *to cut, nick*
**incubo** (*1*) (c. dat), *to lie upon*
**infinitum**, -i, n. *the beyond, boundless space*
**iter**, itineris, n. *passage, journey, progress*
**labor**, -i, lapsus, *dep. to fall*
**lacuna**, -ae, f. *puddle, pool, pond*
**lanius**, -i, m. *butcher*
**longinquus**, -a, -um, *far off, remote, distant*
**lux**, lucis, f. *light*
**mordeo**, -ēre, momordi, morsus, *to bite, sting*
**mulceo**, -ēre, -si, -sus, *to stroke*
**obscurus**, -a, -um, *dim, dark*
**obsecro** (*1*), *to beseech, implore, supplicate*

**offendo**, -ere, -fendi, -fensus, *to hit, bump*
**ops**, opis, *f. aid, help, support*
**oro** (*1*), *to pray, beg*
**os**, oris, *n. mouth; lips*
**paciscor**, -i, pactus, dep. *to make a bargain*
**palpo** (*1*), *to stroke*
**paries**, -etis, *m. wall*
**pendeo**, -ēre, pependi, pensus, *to hang (down), be suspended*
**percutio**, -ere, -cussi, -cussus, *to strike (hard), smite, pierce*
**perscendo**, -ere, *to climb, clamber*
**pictura muralis**, *f. mural*
**pingo**, -ere, pinxi, pictus, *to paint, depict, portray*
**praebeo**, -ēre, -ui, -itus, *to show, exhibit*
**praecido**, -ere, -cidi, -cisus, *to cut off*
**propius**, *adv. closer, nearer*
**quisquis**, quicquid, *whoever, whatever*
**radius**, -i, *m. beam, ray (of light)*
**rapio**, -ere, rapui, raptus, *to seize, grab, snatch*
**recte sedēre**, *to sit straight up*
**repo**, -ere, repsi, reptus, *to creep, crawl*
**resalio**, -ire, -ui, -saltus, *to jump back, leap back*
**resono** (*1*), *to resound, reverberate*
**ritu** (*c. gen*), *in the manner of, like*
**salto** (*1*), *to dance*
**sanctus**, -i, *m. saint*
**sanguineus**, -a, -um, *bloody*
**saxum**, -i, *n. rock*

**semita**, -ae, *f. path, a narrow way*
**se opponere** (*c. dat*), *to face, confront*
**serra**, -ae, *f. saw*
**solum**, -i, *n. ground, floor*
**spelunca**, -ae, *f. cave, cavern*
**spina**, -ae, *f. thorn*
**stillicidium**, -i, *n. drip, trickling liquid*
**supernato** (*1*) (*c. dat*), *to float over; to swim on top*
**tabula**, -ae, *f. slab*
**tardus**, -a, -um, *slow*
**tectum**, -i, *n. roof, ceiling*
**telum**, -i, *n. weapon, spear, shaft*
**tenebrae**, -arum, *f. pl. darkness, gloom*
**tergiversor** (*1*), *dep. to flinch, shift*
**tergum**, -i, *n. back*
**tollo**, -ere, sustuli, sublatus, *to lift, take up; remove*
**tundo**, -ere, tutudi, tunsus, *to strike, thump, bump*
**uncus**, -i, *m. hook*
**viam dare**, *to make way*
**vibro** (*1*), *to brandish*
**vulgus**, -i, *n. the crowd, mob, mass*

# Bios

CAROLYN ADAMS
Carolyn Adams' poetry and art have appeared in *Steam Ticket, Cimarron Review, Evening Street Review, Dissident Voice,* and *Blueline Magazine,* among others. Having authored four chapbooks, her full-length volume is forthcoming from Fernwood Press. She has been twice nominated for both Best of the Net and a Pushcart prize. She is editor and publisher of Red Shoe Press, and volunteers at The Book Corner, a non-profit used bookstore run by the New Friends of The Beaverton City Library.

AJD
AJD has been a sailor, scribe, and bookseller, but started out as an angsty, guilt-ridden child growing up in the American midwest.

A.R. BENDER
A.R. Bender is a writer of German heritage now living in Tacoma, Washington, USA. His short stories, flash fiction, and poetry have been published in numerous literary journals, most recently in: *Pulp Modern, Close To the Bone, Thriller Magazine, Madcap Review, Sein Und Werden, October Hill Magazine,* and *Mystery Tribune.* He's also seeking representation for his completed historical novel. In his spare time, he enjoys hiking off the grid and coaching youth soccer.

ALAN BRICKMAN
Alan Brickman, when not writing, consults to nonprofit organizations on strategic planning and program evaluation. Raised in New York, educated in Massachusetts, he now lives in New Orleans with his 17-year old border collie Jasper, and neither of them can imagine living anywhere else. Alan's work has appeared or is forthcoming in *The Ekphrastic Review, Literary Heist, JONAHMagazine, Variety Pack, Oracle, SPANK the CARP, Streetlight Magazine, Evening Street Press, Sisyphus Magazine,* and *October Hill Magazine.*

AUDRA BURWELL
Audra Burwell is a creative writing major with a strong emphasis on fantasy-themed poetry and fiction that covers universal subject matter. Her work has been published by *Palaver Journal, Deep Overstock, Carcinogenic Poetry, Serpentine Zine Literary Magazine, and Superpresent Magazine,* as well as appearing on the DO Fiction Podcast. She studies at California State University Fresno where she is aiming for a Master of Fine Arts degree. She

is currently employed by Fresno State's Kremen Department as a Communications Assistant.

### Roger Camp

Roger Camp is the author of three photography books including the award winning *Butterflies in Flight, Thames & Hudson, 2002* and *Heat, Charta, Milano, 2008*. His work has appeared in numerous journals including *The New England Review, Phoebe, Folio* and the *New York Quarterly*. His work is represented by the Robin Rice Gallery, NYC. More of his work may be seen on Luminous-Lint.com.

### Carella Keil

Carella is a poet and digital artist who splits her time between the ethereal world of dreams, and Toronto, Canada, depending on the weather. Her work involves themes of mental health, nature and sexuality, often in a surrealist tone. Carella is the recipient of the Stanley Fefferman Prize in Creative Writing (2006) and 2nd place winner in the Open Minds Quarterly BrainStorm Poetry Contest (2017). Recently, she has been published in *OMQ, Margins Magazine, Wrongdoing Magazine* and *Shuf Poetry*.

### Cecily Cecil

Cecily Cecil is a writer of fiction and poetry. She is a current MFA student in Lesley University's fiction program. She previously received her MA in English from Kansas State University. She lives in Manhattan, Kansas, where she enjoys work at her local public library.

### Mickey Collins

Mickey ~~rights wrongs~~. Mickey ~~wrongs rites~~. Mickey writes words, sometimes wrong words but he tries to get it write.

### Deborah Coy

Deborah Coy, former school librarian, has long loved Fantasy and Science Fiction so her poetry often falls into these genres. She has published in multiple anthologies, journals, and online magazines.

### John Delaney

In 2016, I moved out to Port Townsend, WA, after retiring as curator of historic maps at Princeton University. In 2017, I published *Waypoints*, a collection of place poems. *Twenty Questions*, a chapbook, appeared in 2019, and *Delicate Arch*, poems and photographs of national parks and monuments, came out earlier this year.

### Ivan de Monbrison
Ivan de Monbrison is a French poet and artist living in Paris born in 1969 and affected by various types of mental disorders, he has published some poems in the past.

### Mark DeCarteret
Mark DeCarteret has been working at Water Street Books in Exeter NH for 10 years. Worked at Stroudwater Books in Portsmouth for 7. And Wordsworth in Cambridge MA for 1. He's also worked at the Emerson College Library in Boston and volunteered at Wiggin Memorial Library in Stratham NH. His poetry has appeared in 450 reviews, 25 anthologies and 7 books.

### Marie Dolores
Marie Dolores is the pen name I created to spare people the challenge of pronouncing my given name, Dawn Wisniewski. I'm a US born writer currently living in Ireland. I've been writing since my teens as an outlet for the highs, lows, and middle earth moments of my life. Despite a lengthy career in the logical world of information technology I've been able to maintain a tunnel into the creative side of my brain.
I have developed a portfolio of poetry, short stories, a series of fantasy novels in various stages of completion, as well as a historical fiction novel, also in progress.
I've been long and short listed for a number of contests and publications. My poetry publications include *Skylight 47*, *Orbis*, and the *Hysteria 6* anthology. In 2020 I also won first prize in the Dancing Poetry contest.

### Desiree Ducharme
Desiree Ducharme is a writer and dormant dragon who makes a living as an Inventory Manager at Powell's City of Books. She spends her non-work time pretending she won't buy every random mid-century mass market with a ridiculous cover she comes across. You can read more of her writing at desireeducharme.com.

### Lynette G. Esposito
Lynette G. Esposito, MA Rutgers, has been published in *Poetry Quarterly*, *North of Oxford*, *Twin Decades*, *Remembered Arts*, *Reader's Digest*, *US1*, and others. She was married to Attilio Esposito and lives with eight rescued muses in Southern New Jersey.

### Robert Eversmann
Robert Eversmann works for *Deep Overstock*.

## Anna Laura Falvey

Anna Laura Falvey (she/her) is a Brooklyn-based poet and theater-maker. In 2020, she graduated from Bard College with degrees in Classics & Written Arts, with a specialty in Ancient Greek tragedy and poetry. She spent her college career blissfully hidden behind the Circulation and Reference desks at the Stevenson Library, where she worked. Anna Laura has been a teaching artist with Artists Striving to End Poverty since 2019, and is currently serving as an ArtistYear Senior Fellow, teaching Poetry in Queens, NY where she is the resident teaching artist at a transfer high school. Her work has appeared in *Icarus Magazine* as well as in issues 15, 16, & 17 of *Deep Overstock*.

## Kate Falvey

Kate Falvey's work has been published in many journals and anthologies, including four previous issues of *Deep Overstock*; in a full-length collection, *The Language of Little Girls* (David Robert Books); and in two chapbooks, *What the Sea Washes Up* (Dancing Girl Press) and *Morning Constitutional in Sunhat and Bolero* (Green Fuse Poetic Arts). She co-founded (with Monique Ferrell) and edited the *2 Bridges Review*, published through City Tech (City University of New York) where she teaches, and is an associate editor for the *Bellevue Literary Review*.

## Amalia E. Gnanadesikan

Amalia E. Gnanadesikan's poetry has been published in *Vita Brevis, Uppagus, and Spillwords*. She lives with her husband, three cats, and seventeen built-in bookcases in Severna Park, Maryland, where she is learning to make mead. When not at home, she can be found nursing a decaf cappuccino at the bookstore café.

## Clarissa Grunwald

Clarissa Grunwald is a librarian at Elizabethtown College. She has previously been published in *Jet Fuel Review* and *Drunk Monkeys*. When she isn't writing, she enjoys playing viola and pen & paper RPGs.

## Heather Hambley

Heather is a Latin teacher turned translator. She has a BA in Classics from Reed College, where she developed a deep passion for Latin poetry and mythological women, especially Helen of Troy. She currently lives in Central Oregon with her husband Andy and their 15yo doggo Mo. She loves horror movies, particularly anything cozy or campy. Her dream is to translate Latin in the horror space, so hit her up with your spells, spooks, and spoofs. Heather's website is latinklub.wordpress.com.

RILEY HUFF
Since Riley Huff was a young child, when he started folding and stapling together pieces of paper to create miniature books at the age of four, he has loved the power and the folly of the written word. He has contributed articles to *Creative Loafing, DoTheBay,* and *440 Magazine*; fiction to *Balderdash Literary Review*; and poetry to the anthology *2020: An Anthology of Poetry with Drawings* from Black Dog and One-Eyed Press. He is a journalist, poet, comedian, and horror-movie screenwriter based in San Francisco, CA.

MELISSA KERMAN
My name is Melissa Kerman and I'm a writer from Long Island.

CHRISTINE KWON
Christine Kwon writes poetry and fiction in her little New Orleans yellow shotgun house. She is the 2022 winner of the Cowles Poetry Book Prize. Her first book of poems, "A Ribbon the Most Perfect Blue," will be published in late 2023 from Southeast Missouri State University Press. Poems and short stories are forthcoming in blush lit, The Columbia Review, and X-R-A-Y, among other places.

BEE LB
BEE LB is an array of letters, bound to impulse; a writer creating delicate connections. they have called any number of places home; currently, a single yellow wall in Michigan. they have been published in *Revolute Lit, After the Pause,* and *Roanoke Review,* among others. they are the 2022 winner of the Bea Gonzalez Prize for Poetry. they are a poetry reader for Capsule Stories. their portfolio can be found at twinbrights.carrd.co

HERMA S.Y. LI
Herma S.Y. Li is a first-time writer, currently a 15-year-old student about to enter Taipei First Girls High School in Taipei, Taiwan. Her current favorite book is *Tangleweed and Brine* by Deirdre Sullivan. Born in a city filled with rain and mist, she spends her time reading novels, doodling in notebooks, and wandering allays around her home trying to bring about an encounter with good inspiration.

RYAN SHANE LOPEZ
These days, Ryan is an adjunct instructor at Austin Community College and Concordia University, but in past lives, he supported his writing habit through myriad part-time occupations, including that of a lowly bookseller. For some reason, he spent three years earning an MFA, which has debatably helped his writing appear in numerous magazines you've likely never heard

of, including *Hypnopomp, Porter House Review, Lunate, Fudoki, Patheos, Bodega,* and *The Bookends Review*. He lives in Austin, Texas, with his wife, Hannah, and their young children.

JOAN MAZZA
Joan Mazza is a retired medical microbiologist and psychotherapist, and taught workshops focused on understanding dreams and nightmares. She is the author of six self-help psychology books, including *Dreaming Your Real Self*. Her poetry has appeared in *Crab Orchard Review, Prairie Schooner, Slant, Poet Lore, The Nation,* and other publications. She lives in rural central Virginia.

MAUMIL MEHRAJ
Maumil is a writer from Kashmir, and currently, she is studying Conflict Transformation and Peace Building at the Lady Shri Ram College for Women where she is researching Material Memories of Conflict. She also graduated as the Valedictorian of the International Writing Program, hosted by the Iowa University.

KARLA LINN MERRIFIELD
Karla Linn Merrifield has had 1000+ poems appear in dozens of journals and anthologies. She has 15 books to her credit. Following her 2018 *Psyche's Scroll* (Poetry Box Select) is the full-length book *Athabaskan Fractal: Poems of the Far North* from Cirque Press. Her newest poetry collection, *My Body the Guitar*, recently nominated for the National Book Award, was inspired by famous guitarists and their guitars and published in December 2021 by Before Your Quiet Eyes Publications Holograph Series (Rochester, NY). She is a frequent contributor to *The Songs of Eretz Poetry Review*. Web site: karlalinnmerrifield.org; blog at karlalinnmerrifield.wordpress.com; Tweet @LinnMerrifiel; facebook.com/karlalinn.merrifield.

BEN NARDOLILLI
Ben Nardolilli currently lives in New York City. His work has appeared in *Perigee Magazine, Red Fez, Danse Macabre, The 22 Magazine, Quail Bell Magazine, Elimae, The Northampton Review, Local Train Magazine, The Minetta Review,* and *Yes Poetry*. He blogs at mirrorsponge.blogspot.com and is trying to publish his novels.

DANIEL J. NICKOLAS
"Daniel J. Nickolas" is the thinly veiled pseudonym for a bookseller at Powell's on Hawthorne, where he is the (self-appointed, unofficial) head of the science and mathematics sections. One of Daniel's personal goals as a bookseller, and writer, is to help science-curious individuals unearth their

passion for the sciences--a passion he believers every human, consciously or not, holds. He has previously published with *The Pacific Sentinel, Pathos Literary Magazine,* and *The Clackamas Literary Review.* You can find more writing by Daniel at danieljnickolas@wordpress.com

TIMOTHY ARLISS OBRIEN
Timothy Arliss OBrien is an interdisciplinary artist in music composition and writing. He has premiered with The Astoria Music Festival, Cascadia Composers, and ENAensemble's Serial Opera Project. He has published several books of poetry, (*The Art of Learning to Fly, Dear God I'm a Faggot, Happy LGBTQ Wrath Month*), and has written for Look Up Records (Seattle), and *Deep Overstock*: The Bookseller's Journal. He also hosts the podcast The Poet Heroic, and manages the digital magic space The Healers Coven.
He also showcases his psychedelic makeup skills as the phenomenal drag queen Tabitha Acidz.
Check out more at: www.timothyarlissobrien.com

MARK PARSONS
Mark Parsons' poems have been recently published or are forthcoming in *Ex Pat Press, Dreich, Cape Rock,* and *I-70 Review*. He lives in Tokyo, Japan.

JUSTIN RATCLIFF
Justin Ratcliff is a new emerging poet, who was cast into the depths of himself during the Covid-19 outbreak. Born, raised, and still preceding in South Central Alaska. Draws much of his inspirations from psychology, philosophy, theology, nature, and dark fantasy.

CAROLINE REDDY
Caroline Reddy's work has been accepted or published in *Active Muse, Bethlehem Writers Roundtable, Braided Way, Calliope, Clinch, Grey Sparrow, International Human Rights Arts Festival, Literary Heist, The Opiate, Quail Bell* and *Star\*line*, among others. In the fall of 2021, her poem "A Sacred Dance" was nominated for the Best of The Net prize by Active Muse. A native of Shiraz, Iran, Caroline Reddy is working on a collection of poems titled Star Being, which chronicles the life of a Star Seed on earth.

ALEX RICHARDSON
Alex Richardson teaches creative writing, literature, and film at Limestone University. His poems have appeared in over 50 magazines, journals, and anthologies. His first collection, *Porch Night on Walnut Street*, was published by Plainview Press.

FIN RYALS
I worked at Barnes and Noble for a number of months where I held the unofficial title of "resident literary scholar" due to my educational background. I was nonetheless exposed to contemporary works of fiction and poetry that I would not have encountered otherwise. And I take great pride in knowing that I exposed customers to older works of fiction that they too would not have encountered.

MICHAEL SANTIAGO
Michael Santiago is a serial expat, avid traveler, and writer of all kinds. Originally from New York City, and later relocating to Rome in 2016 and Nanjing in 2018. He enjoys the finer things in life like walks on the beach, existential conversations and swapping murder mystery ideas. Keen on exploring themes of humanity within a fictitious context and aspiring author.

LARS STRAEHLER-POHL
Lars Straehler-Pohl is a writer and musician based in Berlin, Germany. The centerpiece of his interdisciplinary work is the perception of presence. He holds a degree in philosophy, psychology and history from the Freie Universität Berlin and was simultaneously educated in Orchestral Conducting and Design Thinking. As a conductor, he has a strong interest in contemporary music and the recovery of forgotten, banned and lost compositions. He re-orchestrated Albéric Magnard's opera "Yolande", which burned with its composer in 1914. The focus of his academic publications and teaching is on aesthetics. In his audio-visual works, he experiments on how a one-time impression can become a long-term memory.

JIHYE SHIN
Jihye Shin is a Korean-American poet and bookseller based in Florida.

ELIZABETH TEMPLEMAN
Elizabeth Templeman, a lover and collector of books, lives, works, and writes in the south-central interior of British Columbia. Publications include individual essays appearing in various journals and anthologies, and two books of essays, *Notes from the Interior,* and *Out & Back, Family in Motion.* To learn more about her, check out her website elizabethtempleman.trubox.ca

ERIC THRALBY
Captain by trade, Cpt. Eric Thralby works wood in his long off-days. He time-to-time pilots the Bremerton Ferry (Bremerton—Vashon; Vahon—Bremerton), while other times sells books on amazon.com, SellerID: plainpages. He'll sell any books the people love, strolling down to library and

yard sales, but he loves especially books of Romantic fiction, not of risqué gargoyles, not harlequin romance, but knights, errant or of the Table. Eric has not published before, but has read in local readings at the Gig Harbor Candy Company and the Lavender Inne, also in Gig Harbor.

Vernon Tremor
Vernon Tremor is a member of the Bremerton Writers Association and a custodian at the observatory. This is his first time publishing and he is quite happy about it. He has been writing in Maev Barba's workshops, deep in the cold, wet woods.

Z.B. Wagman
Z.B. Wagman is an editor for the *Deep Overstock Literary Journal* and a co-host of the Deep Overstock Fiction podcast. When not writing or editing he can be found behind the desk at the Beaverton City Library, where he finds much inspiration.

Olive Wexler
Olive Wexler is a Literary Scout and Writer based in Brooklyn, NY. She graduated from Wesleyan University after studying English and Theatre and is interested in telling stories about the in-between of nostalgia, love, and loneliness. When she's not writing, you can find her dancing in the kitchen with something cooking on the stove.

Nicholas Yandell
Nicholas Yandell is a composer, who sometimes creates with words instead of sound. In those cases, he usually ends up with fiction and occasionally poetry. He also paints and draws, and often all these activities become combined, because they're really not all that different from each other, and it's all just art right?
When not working on creative projects, Nick works as a bookseller at Powell's Books in Portland, Oregon, where he enjoys being surrounded by a wealth of knowledge, as well as working and interacting with creatively stimulating people. He has a website where he displays his creations; it's nicholasyandell.com. Check it out!

*Rights to the works contained in this journal belong to their respective authors. Any ideas or beliefs presented by these authors do not necessarily reflect the ideas or beliefs held by* Deep Overstock's *editors.*

CPSIA information can be obtained
at www.ICGtesting.com
Printed in the USA
BVHW080532151022
649211BV00002B/135